MARK PENN GOES TO WAR

Michael Springer

To Lorraine,
With best wishes,
Michael Springer
2-1-11

A SEQUEL TO "THE BOOTLEGGER'S SECRET"

Outskirts Press, Inc.
Denver, Colorado

Also by Michael Springer

THE BOOTLEGGER'S SECRET

Mark Penn Goes to War
A Sequel to "The Bootlegger's Secret"
All Rights Reserved.
Copyright © 2010 Michael Springer
v2.0

Cover Photo © 2010 JupiterImages Corporation. All rights reserved - used with permission.

Outskirts Press, Inc.
http://www.outskirtspress.com

ISBN: 978-1-4327-6278-0

Outskirts Press and the "OP" logo are trademarks belonging to Outskirts Press, Inc.

PRINTED IN THE UNITED STATES OF AMERICA

To The Memory of My Parents

Tell the men to fire faster, fight
till she sinks, and don't give up the ship.

Captain James Lawrence, USN, mortally wounded
aboard the USS *Chesapeake* (June 1, 1813)

Chapter 1

Mark Penn held his Daisy air rifle chest-high with both hands the way Marines did in the new movie, *To the Shores of Tripoli*. He was tracking the enemy on the Middleton Ridge—using trees, boulders, and caves as cover. Six months had passed since Japan's sneak attack on the U. S. Navy base at Pearl Harbor. Mark was too young to join the Marines and fight the real enemy, but he could play war like millions of red-blooded American kids.

He was alone because his pal Swede Larson was in summer school for flunking sixth-grade geography. How anybody could have trouble with that subject was beyond Mark, but Swede seemed to thrive on trouble.

Ahead was a spring-fed creek that tumbled down the ridge and emptied into the Minnesota River upstream from the boys' treehouse. From here, the river meandered like a gray snake across the green valley floor. He dropped to his knees, splashed his face with the icy water, and had a long drink.

Mark scrambled to his feet and crouched out of the woods into a grassy clearing. He froze at the sight of a lifelike scarecrow dressed in tattered blue overalls. It stood guard in the center of a half-acre garden with neat rows of vegetable seedlings.

Mark heard voices behind him. He flopped to the ground and

rolled behind a fat honeysuckle bush like the tough leatherneck he longed to be.

A man and a girl walked out of the woods toward him. Both were dressed in blue shirts, dungarees, and black work shoes. The girl wore a red bandanna on her head. The man had graying black hair and a gimpy right leg. He said something. She smiled.

Goose bumps rose on Mark's arms as the pair got closer. They looked Oriental. Could they be Japanese? Maybe they were spies. Why didn't they talk some more so he could tell if they spoke English?

The two passed so close that Mark could hear the soft creaking of their shoes. He counted to ten and crawled after them in the tall grass.

Beyond the clearing was a three-foot chain link fence that secured a well-kept yard and white clapboard house that needed paint. The man unlatched a gate, and the pair went up a walk and four steps. Both removed their shoes before going inside.

Mark crept to a lilac bush fifty yards from the house. Why hadn't he brought Swede's telescope?

The front door opened, and the girl skipped down the steps barefooted and bare-headed. Her short black hair was cut in bangs, and her brown eyes had an almond-shape. She was definitely Oriental. Mark had never seen anybody like her.

The girl leaned forward, lobbed a smooth gray stone onto the walk in front of her, and jumped ahead twice on one foot. She was playing hopscotch. Mark could see the white chalklines now. And she was singing "When Johnny Comes Marching Home" in perfect English.

The front door opened again. A tiny Oriental woman with gold-rimmed glasses came outside. Her gray hair was done in a bun, and she wore a flowered cotton kimono. Mark recognized the long gown with the sash and big sleeves from his geography book. They had to be Japanese.

The woman beckoned to the girl, and they went inside.

Mark got to his knees. This wasn't a game anymore. He had to tell somebody. But who'd believe him? His dad? Police Chief Morton? And what would he tell them? That he saw people who looked Japanese, who might be spies? He needed more proof. Mark crawled through the grass toward the back of the house.

Off to the right, at the edge of the woods, was a two-holer out-house. To the left was a weather-beaten shed with the doors hooked open. Inside were a black '39 Ford and a two-wheeled wooden trailer, both with California plates.

President Franklin Roosevelt had ordered that all Japanese on the west coast be sent to internment camps as potential wartime enemies. Maybe these people had skipped out before they could be imprisoned, or maybe they'd escaped from a camp.

A rustle in the grass behind Mark stiffened him. He looked up to face the Japanese man who'd been with the girl. At his side was a brown and blue Doberman pinscher.

"What're you doing here?" The man's English was nasal, but as perfect as the girl's.

Mark's reply came out like a squeak. "Nothing."

"Nothing," the man boomed back. "This is private property. You're trespassing. I could have you arrested."

Mark's brain was spinning. Here was this Japanese man who might be a spy or escaped prisoner talking about having him arrested.

"Did you hear me?"

Mark sat up and edged away as the dog sniffed at his dungaree pantleg. "I didn't mean anything..."

A '41 Chevy pickup came crunching down the graveled driveway. Two small shadows moved behind the kitchen curtains.

The man scowled at Mark. "I don't want to see your face again. Now, get out of here."

Mark glanced over his shoulder every few yards as he scurried to a thick sugar maple at the edge of the woods. He dropped to the ground behind an earthen berm the tree roots had raised, a great place to watch the man approach the truck.

Two men in their early forties dressed in striped overalls and work caps got out of the pickup. One was tall, the other short. Both had bushy mustaches. They reminded Mark of Mutt and Jeff, the cartoon characters.

The taller man took a German Luger out of a baggy back pocket and gave it to the Japanese man. Mark recalled the unusual shape of the pistol—long, thin barrel and angled grip—from *The Invaders*, a movie about Nazis in Canada.

They all spoke together for a minute, then Mutt and Jeff got into the truck, made a U-turn, and drove away.

"Come on, Brutus," the Japanese man said. He patted the Doberman's head as they walked to the back of the house. The man opened a heavy storm cellar door, led the dog down a half-dozen limestone steps, and closed the door behind them.

The twelve-o'clock siren wailed at the Middleton fire station. Swede got out of summer school at noon. His pal would be at the treehouse in a few minutes. Swede would know what to do.

Chapter 2

Mark followed the creek down the ridge, through the culverts under the train tracks and Bottom Road, and along the riverbank to where a ten-foot rope hung among the tree vines. He glanced around in case anybody was watching, then shinnied up the rope and boosted himself through an open trap door into the treehouse.

The hideaway was eight-feet-square, and invisible among the thick leaves of a fifty-foot black oak. Swede and he had built it a year ago with scrap lumber from the abandoned Middleton icehouse. Mark slid his Daisy into the old, wooden foot locker they used for storage and a table.

There was a soft pounding of Keds along the weedy path that followed the river. The treehouse rocked as Swede climbed the rope. He crawled inside and sat at the foot locker opposite Mark.

"Summer school's for the birds. I'm not going back."

"You did fifth grade twice. You want to do sixth twice?"

Swede frowned. He was a year older than Mark, and built like Minnesota football great, Bronko Nagurski. Swede could pass for eighteen, and not a day went by that he didn't calculate ways of getting into the Marines or Army. Lots of underage guys were doing it these days.

Mark got to his knees. "Guess what I saw on the ridge? Japanese."

"Yeah, I saw Superman, too. What were you doing up there?"

"Honest." Mark raised his right hand and told Swede what had happened. "They might be spies. We have to report them."

One of the oak's thick branches had a hollowed-out knot the boys called their "safe." Swede reached inside and pulled out his ten-power Sears telescope. "I want to see for myself."

"The man said not to come back."

"He didn't say it to me." Swede tucked the telescope under his belt, scooched to the edge of the trap door, and slid down the rope.

Mark wasn't going to give Swede a chance to call him chicken. If he had to go back into enemy territory, Swede was the fearless guy he wanted with him.

Mark led the way up the ridge. The boys crept to the maple, lay on their stomachs, and took turns with the telescope.

The Japanese family was seated around a pine picnic table in the front yard. They were eating noodles with chop sticks from blue porcelain bowls. Their conversation was too faint to hear. The dog was snoozing under the table. An orange, three-foot kite shaped like a fish was flying from a bamboo pole stuck in the flag holder by the front door.

Swede elbowed Mark, and gave him the thumbs up. He, too, remembered the kimono—and chop sticks—from his geography book. And Mark was right, they had to tell somebody, but who?

The boys waited a few minutes after the family went inside, then fled down the ridge to the treehouse. They sat in opposite corners breathing hard.

Mark finally said, "We should tell Chief Morton."

"Not me. Last time I saw him, he threatened to send me to reform school."

"What d'ya expect after throwing a cherry bomb under his car?"

Swede grinned. "I've got a better idea. Let's tell your old man and let him tell Morton." He put the telescope in the safe.

Mark agreed. The boys left the treehouse, pulled their bikes out of the weedy ditch along the graveled Bottom Road, and pumped toward town, Mark on his shiny Elgin Red-Bird and Swede on his fenderless old Schwinn.

Tom Penn was the Middleton branch manager of the Hartford Mutual Casualty Company. The boys went to his office on the second floor of the Odd Fellows Building, but Mr. Penn was at lunch with a client and wouldn't return until two o'clock. They decided to have a swim and come back later.

Mark and Swede took their usual short cut across town through the alley behind the Municipal Building. Inside were the police and fire departments.

Just ahead, in the police parking lot, the pear-shaped Chief Morton got out of his unmarked black '41 Plymouth and waddled toward the building's back door. With him was his German Shepherd Fritz, who had most of the town's kids scared. Nobody had ever seen the dog do anything more than growl, but that didn't matter.

"Come on, Swede, there's Morton. Let's tell him." Mark stopped and parked in the bike rack next to the building.

Swede eased alongside. "I hope you know what you're doing."

"Chief," Mark yelled as he ran toward the door.

"I'm busy." Morton kept walking.

"Spies." Mark figured if that didn't get him, nothing would.

Morton stopped and turned around. "Spies?"

The boys nodded and edged forward.

"Honest." Mark crossed his heart. "Japanese. We saw them."

Morton waved the boys inside, down the hallway, and into an empty conference room. They sat at a round oak table. The Chief removed a gray cap that matched his tight-fitting uniform. He was bald except for a fuzzy white fringe around his enormous ears. Fritz circled and settled in a corner.

"All right, let's have it."

Mark told his story. The Chief listened without speaking or changing his sour expression. When Mark was done, Morton moved a brass cuspidor out from under the table with his black boot and spat into it.

"You told anybody about this?" Morton asked.

The boys shook their heads.

"Then don't. Don't you two ever stay home and mind your own business?" He glared at Swede.

Swede's face flushed with anger. "We just thought we were doing our duty reporting that there were Japanese around, like the war poster at the post office says we should."

Morton gave Swede a stiff smile that exposed his snuff-stained teeth. "I know all about them, and they aren't spies."

"What are they then?" Swede said.

"Law-abiding American citizens, like the rest of us." Morton eyed Swede. "Or most of us. Born and raised in the U. S. of A."

"But Chief," Mark said, "I've read about Japanese—and Germans, too—who've been living in this country for years, just waiting for the chance to spy or sabotage the war effort. How do we know these people aren't like that?"

"And what about the guys with the Luger?" Swede said.

Morton frowned and nodded several times. "All right. I'm going to investigate all this, but I want your promise that you won't tell anybody. Nobody. What d'ya say?"

"Can't we help?" Mark said.

"No, no, I appreciate the offer, but I need to handle this my own way. Besides, you've already broken the law trespassing on private property." He eyed Mark. "What would your folks think of that? You two go up there again, and you might not get off so easy."

"But you'll tell us what you find out, right?" Swede said.

"I'll tell you everything I can. Now promise."

The boys promised, but crossed their fingers under the table.

"Good." Morton stood up, put on his cap, and toddled from the room. Fritz was right behind.

"What a waste of time that was," Swede said.

"Yeah, and trying to blackmail me with telling my folks about trespassing."

"Let's give him a week. If we don't hear anything by then, we'll go back up there and do our own investigation."

"I'll ask my dad tonight if he knows anything about a Japanese family in town," Mark said.

"Good idea. He knows everybody. But keep me out of it."

Mark nodded. For a guy who was fearless, Swede sure worried a lot.

Chapter 3

Chief Morton watched through his fly-specked office window as Mark and Swede biked down the alley. Those two were going to poke their noses where they didn't belong once too often.

Morton had considered Swede a prime candidate for Boys Town with an alcoholic old man and sick Ma. Then Alf Larson stopped drinking, quit his job as janitor at the Odd Fellows Building, and hitchhiked to San Diego to build B-24s at Consolidated Aircraft. He was sending home a hundred bucks a week, more than most people in town made. Ernestine Larson had recovered from the nervous breakdown she'd suffered after her baby girl died from diphtheria. And Swede was staying out of trouble. But it couldn't last. None of it.

Morton had two black phones on his cluttered walnut desk, one that went through the police switchboard and another with a private line. He dialed a number on the private phone.

Robert Matsui answered the extension wall phone the FBI had installed in the cellar of his home on the ridge. "Yes?"

"This is Morton. You had a visitor today."

"Several."

"I mean a kid."

"How'd you know about him? Have you been watching us?"

"No, we haven't been watching you. Just listen." Morton related what Mark and Swede had told him. "I warned them to stay away."

"I scared the devil out of the boy I caught. He won't be back."

"Maybe, but you don't know the other one. What's with the Luger?"

"A present from Joe Beck."

"Present. What for?"

"He didn't say."

"That's a Nazi pistol. Don't you think that's suspicious?"

"Lots of soldiers brought souvenir Lugers home after the last war. Does that make them Nazis?"

"Why are you defending them?" Morton said.

"I'm not defending them. The Beck brothers have been good to us. That's more than I can say for most others around here."

Matsui thought back to early March when he'd first met the Becks at the county housing agency where the two were rewiring the building's antiquated electrical system. Joe, the older, taller brother, was an electrician. Fred was a carpenter.

Matsui had been at the counter complaining to the agency director, Ralph Barnes. "I was promised that my family could rent this house on Jefferson, but when we got to town this morning, the owner said he wouldn't rent to Japanese. I'm an American citizen!"

"I'm sorry," the director said, "but there's nothing I can do. It's a free country, and people can rent to whoever they please."

"Do you have anything for my family? We've been on the road for two weeks."

"Sorry," Barnes said. "Try the classifieds in the *Courier*."

The Becks were waiting outside when Matsui returned to his

dusty Ford and overloaded trailer with more bad news for his family.

"Excuse me, I'm Joe Beck." He offered his hand, which Matsui shook. "My brother Fred and I heard what you said in there. Maybe we can help."

"We know how you feel," Fred said. "Lots of German-American families like ours were mistreated during the last war."

"You weren't locked in camps," Matsui said.

"No, but Pa's sawmill was burned down by vigilantes." There had been anger in Fred's eyes.

"If you want a place to live," Joe said, "we've got a house you can have. It needs some fixing-up, so the rent wouldn't be much."

Matsui shook the brothers' hands and introduced his happy family.

The Matsuis moved into the old Beck homestead, a half-mile through the woods from the brothers' new home. The place was dirty and needed paint, but the roof and floors were sound. With the Becks' help, it was soon livable.

The family was hardly settled when Chief Morton used his flashing red light to stop Matsui's Ford on the Bottom Road. He left his police car, opened Matsui's passenger door, and got inside.

"What's this all about?" Matsui said. "I haven't done anything."

"I have a message from the FBI."

"You're not FBI, you're a policeman."

"I'm Police Chief Morton, but I'm also the FBI liaison in this area. The agency is short of men since the war. Do you know Joe and Fred Beck?"

"They're my landlords."

"How'd that come about?"

Matsui explained how he'd met the Becks. Morton had already heard most of the story from Ralph Barnes.

"Noticed anything suspicious about them?"

"Like what?"

"Anti-American talk."

"You mean like complaining that the U. S. government has locked up a hundred-thousand Japanese-Americans in concentration camps? Including my son, John."

"I'd be careful of talk like that, if I were you."

"You're not me. What do you want?"

"The Becks' uncle Heinz was in charge of the local German-American Bund. He was deported to Germany before the war. Joe and Fred took over his property. The FBI thinks they may be picking up where Heinz left off, recruiting citizens of German heritage for sedition against the U.S. government."

"If the FBI thinks the Becks are Nazis, arrest them," Matsui said.

"No evidence. The FBI had an undercover agent in the local Bund who saw a shipment of weapons and explosives. They raided the property after Heinz was deported, but couldn't find anything incriminating."

"What's all this got to do with me?" Matsui said.

"Haven't you ever wondered why the Becks rented that house to you?"

Matsui shrugged. "Because they knew my family needed a place to live."

"Maybe, but I think they rented it to you because they heard your complaints about the way you were being treated by the government, and thought you might be useful. After all, Germany and Japan are allies."

"I'm an American."

"So are the Becks."

"What do you want?"

"Nothing dangerous. Just keep your eyes and ears open. I'm sure as a loyal American, you'll be glad to help."

Matsui recognized blackmail when he heard it, and agreed. He hadn't seen the Becks except when paying the rent, and had almost forgotten about Morton until this phone call.

"Well, try and find out where the Becks got that Luger," Morton said. "It's important. Call me anytime, office or home. We're here if you need us."

"You mean like the Bakersfield police were when kids spit on my daughter?"

"That won't happen here."

Matsui's voice was thin. "I have to go." He hung up.

Morton frowned as he dropped the receiver into its cradle. Japanese-Americans were easy targets because they looked different. There were rumors about Japanese planes, submarines, and sabotage on the west coast. Who was loyal and who wasn't? That's why all those Japanese residents had been packed up and shipped to camps.

At first, the government had allowed Japanese-Americans to relocate voluntarily away from the west coast, but most had nowhere to go. Matsui had a job in Middleton. He moved his family a month before the relocation order was canceled. Those who hadn't relocated went to camps—including the Matsui son, John.

Morton dialed the FBI regional office in Minneapolis on his private line. He asked for Agent Ted Cole, and reported the latest development in what was called "The Nisei Case"—Nisei being the term for an American born of immigrant Japanese parents—citizens like Robert Matsui and his wife, Rose.

When Morton had finished, Cole said, "So, Joe Beck gave Matsui a Luger. There were Lugers in that shipment our undercover agent saw, but that's the least of our worries."

"What d'ya mean?"

"There were all kinds of explosives: dynamite and timers; incendiaries that look like fountain pens; coal bombs that explode when dropped into the boilers of ships, locomotives, factories..."

Morton whistled softly.

"That shipment is still around somewhere, but I'm not going back till I'm sure where. We have to keep the pressure on Matsui. You really think we can trust him?"

"Who knows? He's angry, especially about his son, and I don't blame him."

"What if we upped the ante?"

"Like what?"

"His son. Call Matsui and tell him that the FBI will see about getting the boy out of that camp."

"You mean it?"

"Just tell him."

Chapter 4

The Penn victory garden took up half the back yard. Mark's mom, his big sister Teresa, and little brother Peter had helped plant it, but weeding was his job. Calling it war work didn't increase his enthusiasm. He wondered if that Japanese girl had to weed the big plot on the ridge, and if she called it a victory garden. Victory for who?

As Mark hoed, Swede scoured the city dump for anything made of rubber. President Roosevelt had designated the last two weeks of June for a national scrap rubber drive. Japanese conquests in the Far East had cut off U. S. supplies, so recycled rubber was crucial to the war effort. Payment was a penny a pound. The boys would buy War Stamps with their profits.

Mark rested on his hoe. There hadn't been a letter all week from Cathy Hall, his girlfriend who'd moved to St. Louis last month. Her dad was an Army captain stationed in Iceland. The family was living with Mrs. Hall's mother for the duration. Mark wondered if their romance could survive the separation. Cathy had tons of friends already. Some had to be boys. Mark sighed, kissed the tip of the hoe handle, and went back to work.

Dorothy Penn looked like a model from a Red Cross Volunteer recruiting poster as she walked up the driveway in her light-blue uniform and cap. She and Swede's ma had been rolling bandages and teaching first aid to young girls at the armory. Mrs. Penn exchanged waves with Mark, and went into the house.

Mark took a break at a picnic table under one of two sixty-foot white elms his great-grandpa had planted as saplings in 1858 to celebrate Minnesota statehood. A branch of the other elm skirted his bedroom window. It was perfect for sneaking in and out of the house after curfew.

Mrs. Penn joined Mark with a frosty pitcher of lemonade and two tall glasses. She filled the glasses, and had a sip. Mark downed his in one swallow.

She frowned, and poured him more lemonade. "Your hair is all matted. Have you been swimming in the river?"

Mark ran his fingers through his blond hair. "That's sweat. From weeding." Swimming in the river was taboo. He had to change the subject. "Say, Mom, do you happen to know of any Japanese living in town?"

"Where do you come up with such ideas?"

Mark bit his tongue. He'd ask his dad after supper.

Mrs. Penn was crankier than usual since the war. Running a household was more difficult every day. Sugar was already rationed. Meat, canned goods, butter, gas, coffee, and shoes were next. The military had priority on everything.

Tom Penn got home from work at six. Supper was six-thirty, tonight tuna casserole. Afterwards, while Mrs. Penn and the children did the dishes, Tom stretched out on the living room sofa and read the *Courier*, Middleton's evening paper. The Philco console was on so the family could listen to their favorite Friday night radio programs—*The Lone Ranger, Double or Nothing, Information Please*—and catch any war bulletins.

Later, Mark checked baseball scores in the paper, while his dad dozed. At eight, there was a news flash. Mr. Penn sat up, and Mark moved to his side.

> The Navy Department has announced a great victory over the Japanese fleet which was invading Midway Island, an important military base west of Pearl Harbor. Admiral Chester Nimitz said that the enemy was retreating from the area and that U. S. Naval forces were in pursuit. Enemy losses were said to be heavy, while U. S. losses were light.
>
> The Navy Department also announced that Japanese planes have bombed Dutch Harbor, a Navy base in the Aleutian Islands of Alaska. There are no reports of casualties, but sources say that several Japanese planes were shot down. We now return you to our regular program.

Mr. Penn's expression was grim. "Good news, bad news," he said. "If the Japanese ever took Midway or got a foothold in Alaska..."

"We aren't going to lose the war?" Mark knew he shouldn't ask such a question, but he needed to hear what his dad thought.

Mr. Penn shook his head. "No, but it won't be easy. People think they've got it tough these days with shortages and high prices. I wonder how they'd like to be in a foxhole on Bataan or Wake Island?"

"If the war takes a long time, then you might be drafted." This was Mark's biggest fear.

Tom Penn was thirty-six. Mark had his sandy hair and blue eyes.

Like all adult males, he'd registered for the draft, but was exempt for now because he was married with children.

He squeezed Mark's shoulder. "Let's cross that bridge when we come to it."

Mark nodded and felt better. Now was a good time to ask. "Say, Dad, do you happen to know of any Japanese living in this area?"

Mr. Penn's eyes lit up. "I did hear about a Japanese family a few weeks ago that tried to rent a house across town. Some of the neighbors raised a fuss because of Pearl Harbor, and the landlord turned the Japanese away. Why do you ask?"

Mark told him what had happened. "Chief Morton said they were American citizens, but I'll bet they're spies."

"If Chief Morton said they're citizens, I believe him. And don't you think if they were spies, authorities would have arrested them by now?"

Mark shrugged. "I guess."

"I don't want you bothering those people again. That man was within his rights ordering you off his property."

"Yes, sir."

Mr. Penn smiled and picked up the *Courier*. "You did the right thing reporting what you saw. They might have been spies. Off to bed now."

Mark said goodnight, and went upstairs to his bedroom. It was on the northwest corner of the first house built on Spring Street, a white Victorian with green shutters. He knelt in front of the screened west window. The breeze through the elm leaves was welcome on this muggy night.

Mark knew that America wouldn't lose the war, but he couldn't help worrying. War was full of worries. There was a ten-by-twenty-foot Roll of Honor sign in front of the Municipal Building with the names of almost a hundred local men and women who were serving in the military. Rudy and Herb Brandt had gold stars beside their names. The brothers had been killed aboard the USS *Arizona* at Pearl Harbor.

Red Collins' name was up there. Red was Mark's best adult friend. He was the former second baseman of the Middleton Aces. Mark was the team's batboy, and Swede was a ball shagger.

Red had joined the Navy the first time out of high school in 1926. After his discharge, he played baseball in the Chicago Cubs' farm system and finally made it to the majors. A framed, auto-graphed picture of Red in his Cubs' uniform sat on Mark's dresser.

Red's pa died in 1936, and he came home to run the family farm. When his ma died last September, he sold the farm, re-enlisted in the Navy, and got orders to the aircraft carrier, USS *Yorktown*.

Red was like a big brother, somebody Mark could talk to and who really listened. Mark wrote to Red every week, but hadn't heard from him since April. The Navy didn't tell the public where ships were or what they were doing. Letters were censored, too. Secrecy was important in wartime, but Mark longed to know that Red was safe wherever he was.

Mark wasn't a holy Joe like some guys, but he prayed every night for his family, country, and Red.

Chapter 5

The Aces held practice on Wednesday and Saturday afternoons. Mark wore his spikes and blue cap with the white M to practice, but saved his warm-up jacket and regulation uniform with the number 1 on the back for Sunday games.

Mark worked with Albert Barth, the groundskeeper and clubhouse boy. Albert was a stooped little man of sixty who always had a smelly stogie clamped between his stained teeth and a whiskey flask in his back pocket.

Before practice and games, Mark and Albert chalked the batter's box and foul lines, raked and wet-down the infield, and distributed equipment.

During batting practice, players relayed hit balls to Mark behind the mound, and he fed them to whoever was pitching. Sometimes he pitched. Mark always hit last during batting practice. Today, he smacked one against the left-field fence at the 295' sign to whoops of approval from the players. This was his second year as batboy, and he loved being a part of the Aces' family.

The Aces had won last year's Southern Minny League championship, and finished third in the state tournament. They were still a fine team with Doc Neal pitching every Sunday, but they missed Red Collins, their captain and spark plug.

Doc Neal was a thirty-five-year-old pediatrician who'd pitched with the St. Louis Cardinals' farm system in Columbus while going to medical school at Ohio State. He was 6-4, 210, and had a blazing fastball and nasty curve.

Swede called the right-field ball-shagger's platform his office. It was a wobbly board nailed to the light pole. His job was to return foul balls and home runs to the field.

The local team was sponsored by the Ace Bottling Company, distributors of Home Pilsner and assorted soft drinks. Their opening-day opponents, the Austin Packers, were sponsored by Geo. A. Hormel & Company, makers of SPAM.

A bitter rivalry between the teams had started five years ago. Aces' manager Clancy Anderson and Packers' manager Shanty Dwyer got into a scrap while arguing over a foul ball. Soon, players from both sides were fighting. Chief Morton had deputized extra men today in case of trouble.

New bleachers made possible a record crowd of over four thousand fans, many from Austin. Mayor Kern threw out the first pitch. The managers argued over ground rules during the exchange of lineup cards at home plate, and kicked dirt on each other. Both were warned by the umpire.

Austin pitcher Lefty Hayes was wild, and walked at least one batter in each of the first seven innings, but he'd only given up two hits and no runs. Doc was almost untouchable, too, and the game was scoreless.

There were two out in the bottom of the eighth when the Aces' speedy Tommy Gordon hit a liner over the center fielder's head. Tommy spiked the catcher while being thrown out at the plate, and the two started fighting.

Both dugouts erupted. The managers, instead of breaking up the fight, headed toward each other. The ensuing fracas involved most players on both sides and hundreds in the stands. Mark grabbed a bat in self-defense, and stayed in the dugout.

It took thirty minutes for police and ushers to clear the field. Five spectators were arrested, and the Austin shortstop was taken to the Middleton Clinic with a broken wrist. When the umpire finished ejecting players, the Packers were left with nine men, the Aces only eight.

Catcher Allie New was also the pitching coach and assistant manager. He was called to home plate by the umpire.

"All right, Newsie, I want nine guys on the field to start the ninth in one minute." He squinted at his watch. "If not, I forfeit the game to Austin."

"I need more time than that, ump. I can't get anybody that fast."

"Thirty seconds." The umpire bent over and dusted off home plate with a stubby whisk broom.

Allie took off his cap and slapped it against his thigh. Fans began to boo as he walked toward the Aces' dugout cussing to himself. Policemen edged along the stands, hands on their billy clubs.

Allie stopped, put on his cap, and shouted to his players, "All right, let's take the field. Come on, a little hustle."

Doc approached his catcher. "We don't have enough players."

"Sure we do." Allie smiled and looked past Doc into the Aces' dugout. "Mark, get out here."

Mark ran to where Allie and Doc were standing.

"Get your glove," Allie said. "You're playing second base."

Mark felt shivers roll across his shoulders.

"Hustle up!"

Mark ran into the dugout, grabbed his Billy Jurges glove, and sped to the second-base bag. Allie put on his mask, squatted behind the plate, and signaled for Doc to warm up.

Austin's acting manager charged toward home plate, put his hands on his hips, and stood nose-to-nose with the umpire. "If you let that kid play, I'll protest to the league. He's not on the roster."

The umpire put on his mask. "Play ball."

Mark had participated in the between-inning infield practice and was covering second when Allie threw the ball down. He swept his glove across the bag the way Red used to do and tossed the ball to Doc, who winked.

Austin's strategy was to take advantage of Mark's inexperience. The first batter tried to place the ball in his direction, but fouled out to the big first baseman, Whitey Williams. The second batter dribbled a roller to Mark, who threw him out by twenty feet. Hecklers sent the Packer back to the dugout with his head down. Doc struck out the third batter, and hometown fans gave the Aces a long ovation.

In the Aces' dugout, Allie read the names of the next three batters off the lineup card. "Doc, Mark, and me. Let's get some runs."

Allie took Mark aside as Doc batted. "Hayes has been all over with his pitches, so make him get it in there. A walk's as good as a hit. And squat down a little to make yourself smaller up there."

Doc flew out to left, and Mark was up. He tried to be calm as he took his favorite bat, a Louisville Slugger with Ducky Medwick's signature on it. There was cheering and whistling as he headed for home plate. Swede was waving like a maniac and yelling his name.

Mark smoothed out the deep holes around the plate, then glanced down to the third-base coaching box where Whitey was going through a series of meaningless signs.

A walk's as good as a hit, Mark kept telling himself as he dug in.

The Austin catcher shifted from foot to foot behind Mark, and spat on the plate. "Watch it, kid, Lefty's a little wild today." He pounded his mitt and shouted, "Come on, Lefty, show this babe what you've got."

Mark lost his concentration. Babe. The catcher called him Babe. That's how Babe Ruth got his nickname. Babe Penn.

Smack. The ball hit the catcher's glove head-high and tight. Mark shuddered.

"Ball one," the umpire said.

No more fooling around. A ball thrown that hard could kill a guy. Mark gritted his teeth and eyed the pitcher. He shut out the buzz of the crowd, the high-pitched infield chorus, the raspy chatter of the catcher. Hayes threw. It was in the dirt.

"Ball two."

At third, Whitey was giving the "take" sign. The next pitch was a change-up that Mark saw all the way—the white whirl, red seams, black lettering. He swung with all his might and missed. The ball hit in front of the plate and skidded to the backstop. It would have been ball three.

"Strike one," the umpire said, raising his right arm.

Allie ran out of the dugout. Mark met him at the on-deck circle.

"Sorry, Allie."

"That's okay. He hasn't thrown one anywhere near the plate. Just make him get it over." Allie patted him on the seat of the pants.

Mark stood in again. The next two pitches were in the dirt, and the Aces had a base runner.

Doc was coaching first, and kept Mark close as Hayes tried to pick him off three times in a row.

The first pitch to Allie went back to the screen, and Mark took second base propelled by Doc's urging, "Go, go, go, go, go, slide. Attaboy."

Mark got up, spanked the dust out of his uniform pants, and took a long look around. He was at the center of the world out here, like a bullfighter or Roman gladiator.

Mark took a short lead. The catcher rifled the ball to second, hoping to find him asleep. The throw went over the shortstop's head, and Mark scampered to third.

"Heads-up play, Mark," Whitey said through cupped hands in the third-base coaching box. "Be alert. Watch for a passed ball, but I'll tell you when to go."

Mark nodded, and took a short, tense lead off third. The crowd quieted down, sensing a climax. Swede's piercing whistle rang in from right field.

Lefty Hayes pitched from a full windup. Allie hit a knuckle ball deep to center field. Whitey crouched to Mark's height. His voice was hoarse and strained: "Tag up. Tag up. Don't go too soon. Go when I say go. GO."

Mark didn't wait to see the ball caught. He scored standing up, ending the game. The Aces won, 1-0, and were in first place.

As Mark turned toward the dugout, he was swept into the air by Whitey, and placed on the first baseman's broad shoulders. The rest of the team was right behind, pushing through a cheering crowd into the locker room.

Pails of beer and pop were brought from the refreshment stand. Pat Edwards, the skinny sports writer from the *Courier*, interviewed Clancy and several players, including Mark.

"Were you scared out there, Mike?"

"Mark."

"Were you scared out there, Mark?"

"No."

"How come?"

Mark shrugged. No wonder players made fun of Edwards. The guy was a nincompoop.

Jake Archibald, the play-by-play announcer for KMIN, asked Mark how it felt to score the winning run. He was on the radio.

"Great."

"What were you thinking about out there?"

"About Red. Red Collins."

"He means the old second baseman of the Aces, who's in the Navy, fans. What about Red?"

"I was just wishing Red was here playing instead of fighting the Japanese."

"You did it for Red, right?"

Mark nodded. "For Red."

"He'd be proud of you, kid."

As Mark backed away from the microphone, Tommy and Allie grabbed him hand-and-foot, hauled him to the showers, and gave him a long soaking. Players only did this on special occasions to guys they liked. Mark yelled and kicked and loved every second.

The park was deserted when Mark and Swede left the locker room. Swede nudged Mark. "Got a present for you." He gave Mark a baseball.

"What's this? You didn't swipe it?"

"Have a look."

Mark turned the ball in his hands. There in blue ink was Clancy's signature, Doc's, Allie's, the whole team. And the date, June 7, 1942. "Where'd you get it?"

"Thought you should have a souvenir. I asked the team for autographs while you were finishing up your chores with Albert."

"Geez, Swede, thanks a lot."

"What're best buddies for?" Swede gave Mark a soft jab on the shoulder.

Chapter 6

Monday's *Courier* ran a banner headline on the sports page:

BATBOY BEATS PACKERS, 1-0
Did It For Red Collins

Mark's name was mentioned eight times in the article, and there was a photo taken in the locker room that really looked like him. He pasted the page in his scrapbook of special events, which until now had been about the war. He'd get extra copies for Cathy and Red.

For the first time in his life, Mark had a sense of immortality. His name would be in the box score forever. It wasn't much compared to, say, Babe Ruth, but not bad for a twelve-year-old.

The only ones not impressed with Mark's new fame were his sister and brother. Teresa was thirteen, pigtailed, and gangly. Peter was ten and a spoiled crybaby—just like Mark used to be, Teresa was going to say once too often. At least they kept out of his and Swede's hair. Their weekday mornings were spent in swimming and life-saving classes at the YMCA, and afternoons at the Sibley Park summer-activities program, which offered everything from sewing to basket weaving.

With Mrs. Penn at Red Cross, Teresa made lunch for them, usually peanut butter and jelly sandwiches.

Mark believed that Teresa spent half her life thinking up ways to make him miserable. Today, she really bushwhacked him. "Did you know that Howard Larson has a girl friend?"

Mark was stunned, but cool. "Don't you know you're not supposed to spread rumors in wartime?"

"It's not a rumor. I saw him having a Coke with Jane Ostrum at the Candy Shoppe yesterday."

"Me, too," Peter said through a mouthful of sandwich.

"So what? Swede told me all about it."

"Thought you said it was a rumor, smarty." Teresa made a face at Mark.

"Anything you say about Swede is a rumor, and don't let him catch you." He turned to Peter. "You, too, pip-squeak."

Mark gobbled his sandwich, gave Teresa her dirty look back, and biked to Aces' practice. If Swede had a girl, why hadn't he said so? Best buddies shared everything, didn't they?

Jane Ostrum was fourteen and built like that blonde bombshell actress, Mae West. Cathy was prettier than Jane, but didn't have much of a figure.

Mark waited until after practice in the locker room to confront Swede. "I hear you're seeing Jane Ostrum."

Swede frowned. "Can't a guy even talk to a girl? Let's have a swim."

Swede had never dated a girl before, and was sensitive about it. Everything had happened so fast. Jane was waiting for her brother Ned, who was also in summer school. They said hi, and the next thing he knew he'd asked her to have a Coke. Or had she asked him? Jane had played footsie with him under the table, and they had a date the next day after school. Swede's heart was still fluttering. If this was love, he wanted more.

Chief Morton was standing by the bike rack when the boys came out the front gate. He'd been talking to Aces' owner Dan Lee about keeping the players under control for next Sunday's game.

"Morning, Chief," Mark said as the boys mounted their bikes.

"You two been keeping out of trouble?" Morton looked grouchy, as usual.

They nodded.

It had been a week since Morton promised to investigate the Japanese family. Swede decided to be bold. "Any news about...the people on the ridge?" he said.

Morton glanced around, then spoke in a hoarse whisper. "I thought we weren't going to talk about that."

"You said you'd tell us what you found out," Swede said.

Morton hunched forward and beckoned to them with wags of his index finger. "Well, I guess there is something I can tell you."

The boys rolled their bikes toward him.

Morton spoke through his teeth. "If I hear one word that you've been bothering those people, I'll have your asses in a sling. Do I make myself clear?"

The boys nodded as they backed away.

"Good. Now, let's change the subject." He gave Mark a crooked smile. "Congratulations on the game Sunday. I guess we showed those Packers where to get off." He slapped Mark on the shoulder, got into his Plymouth, and drove away.

Swede was so angry that his face was deep red. "Who does he think he is?"

"The police chief, that's who." Mark was angry, too, but he wasn't taking it personally. "I'm not going up there, Swede. My dad..."

"Well, go home and play dolls with your sister then. I'll go alone."

Swede pushed off and pumped toward the Bottom Road. Mark hesitated a moment, then caught up with his pal.

Swede spoke in a low, hard voice. "How come he's so hot about keeping us away from there. Must be some big reason."

"I don't know, but that dog was big enough reason for me."

"Yeah, well, we'll stay in the woods this time, just in case."

"Let's smear our faces with mud—like commandos—so nobody can recognize us."

Swede gave Mark the thumbs up.

Swede got his telescope, and the boys slipped to the riverbank. They darkened their faces with the foul-smelling blue mud that early French explorers thought was copper ore, then climbed the ridge and lay on their stomachs behind the raised berm of the maple.

The boys checked out the area with the telescope. The car was gone, but the trailer was in the shed. The drapes were closed. The place looked deserted.

Swede elbowed Mark. "Let's circle the house, but stay in the woods."

Mark nodded. "Watch for that dog."

They were crouching through the rolling woods north of the outhouse when Swede stopped and pointed. "What's that in there?"

Half-hidden among the hillside underbrush was a four-by-six-foot limestone structure. Poison sumac vines covered the moss-stained walls. The word BECK was carved in six-inch letters above a weathered oak door. The boys crept forward through the knee-high grass.

Mark tripped over a gray granite slab. "It's a graveyard."

"Graveyards don't scare me." Swede went to the door and rattled a tarnished brass knob. "Locked." He put a shoulder to the door and grunted. It didn't budge.

Mark was checking the names and dates on the stones. "Looks like a family cemetery. Most of the names are Beck."

"Wonder what's inside?" Swede said.

"Bodies, what else? There's tire tracks along here. Maybe from a funeral."

"Let's see if anybody's home." Swede knocked on the door and listened for a moment. "Guess not."

"Come on, Swede, don't fool around. Let's have a swim."

The boys left the graveyard, and followed the creek down to the river.

Joe Beck opened the mausoleum door, edged outside, and looked around. He didn't know who those nosy kids were, but figured they were lucky. If Fred had been here, they might have wound up as the only non-family members in the cemetery.

Mark and Swede left their clothes on the bank, plunged into the cool water, and swam forty yards to the "point," a mid-river sandbar beyond which the faster, more dangerous current flowed. They rinsed the mud off their faces, then stretched out to soak up the late-afternoon sun.

Swede kicked at Mark's ankle. "You know, I used to say things about you and Cathy. I didn't mean anything bad."

"Uh-huh."

"Guys can see girls and still have pals. Right?"

"Right."

"Too bad Cathy moved away. We could do stuff together."

"Yeah."

"Maybe Jane can find a girl for you. She's got lots of friends."

Mark made a little gravelly sound in his throat that didn't mean yes or no. He wasn't interested in any girl besides Cathy. "Jane's nice."

Swede grinned. Jane was nice, the nicest thing that ever happened to him.

The four-o'clock freight whistled as it left the Middleton yard. It was time for Mark to weed the garden, and Swede to look for more rubber at the city dump.

The boys dressed and biked toward town. Mark waved good-bye as he glided into the Penn driveway. Swede waved back and pumped down Spring Street.

Mark marveled again at how lucky he was to have Swede as a friend. Come hell or high water—Jane, Cathy, anything.

His sense of well-being was shattered when he picked up the *Courier* on the front steps and read the page-one headlines:

LEAGUE ORDERS REPLAY OF PACKERS GAME
Use of Batboy Illegal

Southern Minny officials had ruled that Mark was an ineligible player because his name wasn't on the Aces' roster. The ninth inning would be replayed at a future date.

So much for immortality.

Chapter 7

There was a letter from Cathy the next morning. Mark slipped the pink envelope down his shirt front, and pumped to the treehouse where he could savor it.

He sat cross-legged at the foot locker and sniffed the envelope. No perfume. No S.W.A.K. on the back flap either. His heart skipped a beat.

Mark opened the envelope, took out the delicate pink sheet, and read:

> *Dear Mark,*
>   *This is the hardest letter I ever had to write.*

The words blurred. It was a Dear John letter! Servicemen got them from girlfriends, but Mark never dreamed he'd get one. He read on:

> *We live so far apart, and probably won't see each other until the war is over, and who knows when that'll be. So, I'm freeing you from your promise to wait for me, and hope you'll do the same. Please don't be angry.*
>   *Your friend,*
>   *Cathy Hall*

Your friend. After all they'd meant to each other. Oh God, how could Cathy do this to him?

Mark didn't tell anybody, didn't even answer Cathy's letter. He was too hurt and embarrassed. It would be weeks before he could think of her without pain; but by day's end, Mark had made an irrevocable decision: he was through with girls forever.

Chapter 8

Even the dawn seemed patriotic on Flag Day, layered with red sunlight, white clouds, and blue sky. KMIN's *Early Bird* newscaster reminded listeners, "Red sky in the morning; sailor, take warning." He said there was a fifty-fifty chance that the Aces-Rochester game and the big parade could be rained out.

This year, because of the war, Flag Day had been expanded into a community project to sell War Bonds. The campaign had taken on a greater urgency with news that Japan had invaded the Aleutian Islands of Attu and Kiska. American soil had been occupied. Minnesota didn't seem so safe anymore.

The Navy Department had also revealed the sinking of the aircraft carrier *Lexington* in the Battle of the Coral Sea on May 8. Now more than ever, purchases of War Bonds were needed to buy ships, planes, and guns to defeat the enemy.

Main Street was closed to traffic and decorated with flags and bunting. Loudspeakers on lamp posts stirred the patriotic blood with Army, Navy, and Marine Corps marches. By mid-morning, crowds were larger than those that had greeted President Roosevelt during a 1940 re-election stop.

Businesses were open on this humid Sunday, gung ho to sell War Bonds along with their regular merchandise. Mr. Penn had set up an insurance booth outside the Odd Fellows Building. He gave Mark and Swede each a dollar to buy War Stamps.

Photographs of military men and women were displayed with flowers and flags in store windows. There was an old one of Red Collins in his dress blues and flat hat in the Candy Shoppe.

The Aces beat Rochester, 9-1. Dan Lee donated the day's receipts to the War Bond campaign. Other businesses had similar projects.

Mark and Swede watched the parade from the roof of the Odd Fellows Building. Red, white, and blue floats and flag-draped convertibles showcased beauty queens, politicians, and servicemen home on furlough. Uniformed military, school, and fraternal bands played marches, fight songs, and polkas. Shriners in their satin finery and red fezes sidled and pranced on palominos fitted with tooled leather and ornate silver. Clowns turned somersaults and tossed candy to children. Coeds from Middleton State College sold kisses for a dollar's-worth of War Stamps.

The rumors came like whispers, the facts like thunder. Flag Day had been the backdrop for the largest robbery in Middleton's history.

Two men in Halloween skeleton costumes had hijacked the armored truck from the First National Bank that was picking up War Bond proceeds in the alley behind the Sears, Roebuck store. Bank guard Horace Evans had been shot in the left arm, and taken to St. Luke's Hospital.

Estimates of loss ran to fifty thousand dollars. A one thousand dollar reward was being offered for the capture of the Flag Day Traitors, as the robbers were being called. The good news was that two hundred thousand dollars was safe in the bank, and more was being collected.

Thunderstorms held off until sunset, and left the western ridge crimson. "Red sky at night; sailor's delight," as KMIN's *Nightcap* newscaster told his listeners.

Chapter 9

Old-timers were comparing the Flag Day Traitors to the Jesse James gang, which had robbed another First National Bank in Northfield, Minnesota, sixty-six years ago. All of the gang except Jesse and Frank James had been killed or captured. The two gunmen in Halloween costumes had vanished. A new legend was being born.

Mark was kneeling at the treehouse foot locker working on a letter to Red about the robbery. When Swede got out of school, they'd turn in their scrap rubber. If Swede showed up. Yesterday, he'd had a date with Jane, and didn't get to the treehouse until late-afternoon.

"Dear Red," Mark wrote on some of his dad's office stationery. "Big news." He chewed on the eraser, then tossed the yellow pencil aside.

Red was risking his life fighting the Japanese enemy thousands of miles from home, and there were Japanese right here who might be spies or escapees from an internment camp. Another week had passed since the boys were on the ridge. It was time to go back. And he'd do it alone.

Half an hour later, Mark crouched up the ridge with his Daisy in one hand and Swede's telescope in the other. He lay behind the berm of the maple and surveyed things. The car and trailer were in the shed, but there was no sign of anybody.

The soft creaking of shoes behind Mark jolted him. Why hadn't he been more careful? If that Japanese man caught him again, it'd be curtains.

Mark twisted his body around. Standing beside him was the Japanese girl.

"Boo!" she said. "You're the boy my father chased away the other day, aren't you?"

Mark tried to boost himself into a sitting position, but his arms were like rubber.

"What's the matter, cat got your tongue?" The girl stared at him, then covered her mouth with her hand and giggled. "I saw your picture in the paper. You're the Aces' batboy. What's your name again?"

Mark told her his name. Name, rank, and serial number, nothing else. He sat up. "What's your name?" The war posters said, "Know Your Enemy."

"Ann Matsui. What're you doing here?" She kicked the telescope aside. "Spying on us?"

What was she doing accusing him of spying? If anybody was a spy, it was her father. Where was he? Mark looked around, then stood up. "How long have you lived here?"

"Since March. We came from Bakersfield, California."

"How come you moved to Minnesota?"

The girl hesitated. "My father's work."

"What's he do?"

"He's a chick sexer."

"What's that?"

"He works at the Middleton Hatchery, and separates female

chicks from males."

"Why?"

"So they can tell which ones lay eggs."

"Why?"

"You don't know very much, do you?"

"I never heard of such a job."

The twelve-o'clock siren sounded at the fire station.

"My father said he'd be home for lunch at noon. You'd better go. If he caught you up here again, he'd probably chop your head off." She ran her index finger across her throat.

Mark picked up his Daisy. "He'd have to catch me first."

"I caught you." She turned and headed toward the back of the house.

"You were lucky," Mark shouted as he hightailed it toward the creek.

Ann opened the door to the back porch, and the Doberman slipped outside. She clapped her hands. "Go meet Papa, Brutus." The dog raced toward Mr. Matsui, who was walking in the woods along the path from the Becks' house.

A few minutes earlier and her father would have seen that boy. Ann smiled. He wouldn't have cut Mark's head off, but there was a pair of samurai swords in the cellar that probably had been used that way by her great-grandfather in Japan.

Mark was the first person her own age Ann had talked to since moving to Minnesota. She loved her teddy bear, but he was no substitute for real friends. All of her Japanese classmates and neighbors were in camps. Papa'd had letters about the crowded barracks, barbed wire and guards, hot dusty climate. Ann sighed. Things could be worse.

Maybe she could be friends with that boy, if he ever came back.

He looked scared to death. If he did come back, she'd try to be friendlier.

Rose Matsui called to Ann, and she went inside to set the table for lunch.

A half-mile away, Karl Morton drove his own black '39 Oldsmobile north on the Bottom Road, stopped at the mailboxes marked BECK and MATSUI at the foot of Sawmill Road, then headed up the pot-holed trail. At the top on the right, just before the DEAD END sign, were the steel-mesh gate and six-foot cyclone fence that guarded the Becks' gray clapboard house and garage. To the left was a dirt road to the Matsuis' place.

The Chief stopped his car in the Matsui driveway and got out. He was dressed in brown slacks, a flowery shirt, and smoked glasses.

Mark had gotten halfway down the ridge before missing the telescope. Swede would have his hide. He tore back to the maple.

Matsui paused by the maple. He saw the telescope glinting in the sun and picked it up. It must belong to Ann or John, but wasn't familiar. He told Brutus to stay, and went to meet Morton.

Mark skidded to a halt behind a basswood when he saw the dog sitting under the maple. Then he spotted Matsui with the telescope. The old man was talking to Chief Morton. Mark had never seen Morton out of uniform before. The two men were too far away to hear anything, and he didn't dare move closer because of the dog.

Matsui spoke in a low voice. "You think it's smart coming up here? The Becks are home. They might see you."

"I've been trying to phone you. Thought you were going to keep in touch."

"I've been busy at work. They've got me on overtime."

"But not today, I see."

"It's my afternoon off." Matsui wouldn't tell Morton that he was meeting with a lawyer who thought he might be able to get John out of that camp.

"You hear about the Flag Day robbery?" Morton said.

"I saw it in the paper."

"Not everything was in the paper. The bank guard was shot with a Luger. Joe Beck gave you a Luger."

Matsui stuck out his jaw. "Are you accusing me?"

"I came up here to have a look at it."

"The pistol hasn't been fired. If you don't trust me, get somebody else to spy on the Becks."

"You haven't been much help."

"Neither has the FBI with my son."

The men glared at each other for a moment, then Matsui said, "Listen, I've been riding to work with them every day, but they haven't said or done anything suspicious. You do know that they've started working at the Colt .45 factory?"

Morton's mouth opened in surprise.

Middleton Manufacturing Company had built farm equipment before the war. It was being converted to the production of Colt .45 pistols for the military. The new plant was scheduled to open in mid-July.

Matsui was astounded that Morton didn't know where the Becks were working. Maybe the FBI didn't care about the Becks. Maybe all this cloak-and-dagger business was just a ploy to keep him and his family under surveillance.

Mrs. Matsui waved from the kitchen window.

"Time for lunch," Matsui said. "I don't think you should come up here again."

Morton nodded. "But don't forget, we still have a deal." He got into his car and drove away.

Matsui tapped his thigh with the telescope, and whistled for the Doberman. The dog loped to his side, and the pair entered the house through the cellar door.

Mark sagged against the rough bark of the basswood. He'd never get Swede's telescope back.

Chapter 10

On the way down the ridge, Mark worked out a plan to replace Swede's telescope. As batboy, he had first dibs on cracked bats. Lots of guys would give their right arm for a Louisville Slugger. He'd ask around.

Swede spoiled Mark's scheme before it started. He was slouched against the foot locker with his arms crossed when Mark boosted himself through the trap door.

"You take my telescope?" he snapped.

Mark nodded, put his Daisy on the foot locker, and sat beside Swede.

"Well, where is it?"

What to tell and what to leave out was the problem. Mark couldn't reveal how Ann got the drop on him, but he did tell Swede everything else.

By the time Mark finished, Swede's anger had been replaced by an excited glow. "Can you get out tonight?"

"Sure. My folks are going to a movie, won't be home till late. Why?"

"We're going to rescue my telescope."

"What? That's stupid."

"No, what's stupid was losing my telescope. I should make you go alone, but I'm going to do you a favor—I'm going with you."

"We can't just break into somebody's house. If we get caught, they'd send us to reform school."

"You mean, they'd send me to reform school. Guys like you never go."

Mark shook his head. "I can get you a new one. I've got a plan."

"I don't want a new one. I gave Rich Higgins ten rainbow glassies and my red suede marble bag for that telescope. It's the neatest thing I ever had."

"Okay," Mark said, knowing it was hopeless to argue. "What time?"

"Pick you up at eight. By the time we get up there, it'll be dark."

Mark shook his head.

"You shake your head too much, it'll fall off. We'll go in the cellar, get the telescope, and zip right out. Unless you want to go to the front door?"

"Mark's "no" was a whisper.

"Me neither." Swede grinned, and edged toward the trap door. "Come on, let's turn in our rubber. I'll bet we've got five hundred pounds."

The boys hauled the rubber from the Larson back yard in their Flying Arrow wagons tied behind their bikes. Swede's estimate was high. The scale at Carlson's Shell Station registered four hundred and forty pounds. At a penny a pound, they each received enough for twenty-two dime War Stamps.

Mark worried all afternoon. Being Swede's pal was getting dangerous. Red had warned that Swede would get him into trouble someday, but Mark hadn't listened. The alternative was to break off the friendship. He could never do that.

Swede wasn't worried, but he did foresee two problems: the Japanese family might be home, and there was no telling where the telescope might be. The important thing was to avoid unnecessary risk.

At eight, Mark slipped out of his bedroom window onto the branch of his great-grandpa's elm and swung to the ground. Swede was waiting with two flashlights. A full moon, baffled by scattered clouds, lit their way up the ridge, past the maple, and behind the lilac. The Matsui house was dark, except for a small light over the back porch.

Swede whispered, "No car. No sign of the dog. They must be gone. This'll be easy. Come on."

They crept to the east side of the house. Swede lifted the horizontal oak door by its steel handle and leaned it against a post.

The boys stooped down six limestone steps and through a second vertical door into the musty cellar. They turned on their flashlights. The floor was concrete. The ceiling beams were braced by thick stanchions. Redwood barrels and cardboard boxes sat on a low workbench along an outside wall.

"Gotcha." Swede snatched up his telescope, which was lying on one of the boxes. He waved it at Mark, then tucked it under his belt. "Easy."

"Now, let's get out of here." Mark moved toward the door.

"Not so fast. Wonder what's in these boxes and barrels?"

"Come on, Swede, you said we'd get the telescope and go."

"You go. I'm checking these boxes. Might be some clues."

Mark returned to Swede's side.

Swede opened the nearest box, which contained a U. S. Army khaki uniform. He held up the jacket. It had sergeant's stripes and two rows of ribbons.

"Wonder what a Japanese is doing with this?" Swede put the jacket back.

"How would I know? Let's go."

Swede ignored Mark, and opened the other boxes. They were full of clothing. The barrels were empty.

"Satisfied now?" Mark said.

Swede swung his flashlight across the room. "Let's see what's over there."

He led Mark past a coal furnace and steep steps. In a corner was an oak chair and matching desk with a bronze swivel lamp. Swede switched on the light. Mounted above the desk was a telephone.

The boys froze at the sound of a car engine drifting though the open doors.

"They're home," Mark said. "Let's go."

"Wait till they're inside, so we don't run into anybody."

Car doors slammed. People were talking. A dog barked.

Mark's voice trembled with fear. "The dog."

"We have to chance it." Swede took the telescope from under his belt.

A door closed above them. Floorboards creaked. A hand pump squeaked and water ran. Muffled voices sounded.

They both jumped when the telephone rang. It rang again. Swede unhooked the receiver and listened for several seconds, then he frowned and hung up.

Swede put his hand on Mark's shoulder and whispered, "Let's scram."

The boys edged out of the cellar and into a back yard now lit by a powerful light on a tall post near the shed. They dove for cover behind a rain barrel at the corner of the house.

The Doberman was wandering across the yard away from them. He walked stiffly up to the lilac, lifted his leg, and peed.

The door to the back porch opened. Ann put her little fingers into the corners of her mouth and whistled.

The dog ambled to the porch and went inside. Ann followed. The yard light went out.

"Go," Swede said.

Mark led Swede to the maple, where they caught their breath.

Swede jabbed Mark in the back and chuckled. "She whistles better than you do."

The yard light went on again. The boys started down the ridge as the dog came out of the cellar. Matsui was right behind with a double-barreled shotgun.

"Sic 'em," Matsui said. The dog bounded toward the woods.

The boys careened down the ridge. Swede fell when his telescope caught in a bush. Mark helped him up just as the wide arc of a flashlight swept the hillside. The light went out for a moment, then two shotgun blasts sounded.

Mark let out a little cry of fear. Swede thought that if combat was like this, he'd stay home with Jane.

The boys stumbled the rest of the way to the treehouse, climbed up the rope, and sat in the dark, panting and listening. Swede finally got to his knees and stared out the west window into the darkness. He whispered, "We made it."

"You think he got a look at us?" Mark turned on his flashlight, and stood it upright on the foot locker.

"Too dark. Something set him off though."

"Maybe you monkeying with that phone. What'd you hear?"

"Some guy calling those Japanese every name in the book. He told them to get out of town or he'd burn their house down."

"It must be hard being who they are."

"Yeah, so what?" Swede said. "It's hard being who I am, too."

Despite his bravado, Swede was having second thoughts. What if something had happened to him tonight. His ma would have another nervous breakdown, or worse. Mark was right, going into that house had been stupid. It was time to start thinking before he acted.

Mark was having similar misgivings. Next time Swede suggested something dangerous, he'd say no.

Chapter 11

Rose and Ann Matsui had gone to bed. Robert Matsui sat at the kitchen table in the dark massaging his right thigh. The shrapnel Army doctors had left behind was twitching, and it hurt like the devil.

He was getting too old to be chasing after a couple of hoodlums. Nothing was missing in the cellar. Nothing worth taking. Two shotgun blasts in the air should keep them from coming back. To be safe, he'd turn on the porch and yard lights at night from now on, and get new locks for all doors.

They were cowards, like the one who'd made the vicious phone call. Rose and Ann hadn't heard the foul language and threats this time, but they'd seen his face and knew what was happening. There'd been similar calls in California.

He foolishly thought they'd be safe here. When John got out of that camp, they'd leave. Where could they go? It was open season on Japanese-Americans.

Rose suffered in silence. The war had turned her hair gray. A husband was supposed to protect his family, but he was helpless. Henry Sano, a childhood friend, had hanged himself in the Manzanar camp in California. If happy-go-lucky Henry had lost faith, what hope was there for any of them?

Matsui sighed, and went upstairs to Ann's bedroom. He kissed her cheek and whispered, *"Oyasumi-nasai, Ann-chan.* Goodnight, my dear Ann."

Half-asleep, Ann hugged her teddy bear and whispered, *"Oya-sumi-nasai, Papa-chan."*

Chapter 12

The Aces traveled to Waseca on Sunday and defeated the Braves, 12 to 1. Whitey Williams hit a grand slam and Doc Neal pitched a three-hitter.

A week later, the game at Winona was rained out: two hundred and sixty round-trip miles in the team bus on bumpy Highway 14. And that didn't include two hours in the flooded dugout waiting for the umps to call the game.

Mark was still sore from the bus ride the next morning as he sat on the front porch checking baseball scores and standings in the Minneapolis *Tribune*. The Yankees and Dodgers led the American and National Leagues. Boston slugger Ted Williams had joined the Navy Reserve, but would play the rest of the season. More players were being drafted every day. Aces' center fielder Tommy Gordon had taken his Army physical, and could be called to active duty anytime.

Mark looked up as Clancy Anderson's gray '36 Pontiac braked to a squeaky stop at the front curb. The manager got out and trudged toward the house. What did he want? Had Albert been bad-mouthing him again? Mark braced himself for the worst as he tossed the paper aside and went to the door.

"Hello, Mark," Clancy said. "Your ma or pa home?" His face was pale.

"My mom's washing clothes in the cellar. Come in. Anything wrong?"

Clancy took off his straw hat and went inside. "Would you call her, please?"

Mark nodded. He'd never seen Clancy so subdued. Something was really wrong.

He called his mother, and paced in the living room while she and Clancy talked on the porch. After a few minutes, Mrs. Penn came into the living room.

"Mr. Anderson has something to tell you, Mark."

"What's wrong?" He'd been fired as batboy. That had to be it.

"He'll tell you."

Clancy was waiting in one of the wicker chairs. Mark sat across from him.

"I'm afraid I have some bad news, Mark. I just had a call from Frank Collins, you know, Red's brother in Minneapolis. He got a telegram from the War Department. Red was...killed in action."

"No." Mark squeezed his eyes shut.

"I know what good pals you were, so I thought I'd tell you myself." Clancy gave a little sob, and patted Mark's knee. "I'm sorry."

Tears streamed down Mark's cheeks, but he didn't care who saw him bawling. Red was dead.

Mark stumbled over Clancy's feet on the way to his room. He fell on the bed and cried.

Mrs. Penn followed him upstairs, and sat beside him. "I'm so sorry."

She rubbed his shoulder, but he twisted away. "Don't."

Mrs. Penn got up and left the room with tears in her eyes.

Red Collins was killed on June 4, 1942, aboard the USS *York-town* during the Battle of Midway. The sinking of "The Fighting

Lady" three days later was kept secret by the Navy Department until mid-September 1942 for reasons of national security and morale.

Red's photograph and obituary appeared on page one of the *Courier*:

> *The War Department has announced that Navy Gunner's Mate Second Class James Edward Collins, 33, of Route 2, Middleton, was killed in action in the performance of his duty. His parents were Patrick and Emily Collins, now deceased. He is survived by a brother Frank, sister-in-law, and two nieces. A memorial service will be held at St. Mary's on July 1 at 9 a.m.*

Everybody who knew Red assumed that he'd been aboard *Yorktown* when he was killed. They didn't know for sure until three months later when Red's division officer wrote a brief letter of condolence to Frank Collins. There were no details, just that Red had died upholding the finest traditions of the U. S. Navy. Bronze Star and Purple Heart Medals had been awarded and would be sent to Frank.

Yorktown had been crippled by bombs from Japanese carrier planes in the victorious Battle of the Coral Sea in May 1942, and limped back to Pearl Harbor for emergency repairs. Three days later, the carrier sailed as part of two task forces to intercept a powerful Japanese armada that planned to invade Midway Island and destroy the American fleet. The enemy outnumbered the U. S. in ships, 160-76, and in carriers, four to three. A Japanese victory would leave Hawaii and perhaps the western United States open to invasion.

Neither fleet came within sight of the other. All fighting was done by carrier planes and ships' antiaircraft batteries. After three hours under attack, *Yorktown* had been hit by three bombs and two torpedoes. She was dead in the water, listing twenty-five degrees to port, and vulnerable to further attack.

Red Collins was leading a five-man fire-control party below deck when the first torpedo ripped through *Yorktown's* port side. The explosion riddled the men with steel splinters. They were blinded by flames, choked by smoke, and charred almost beyond recognition. Five brave men lay where they fell as the captain ordered, "Abandon ship."

By some miracle, *Yorktown* was still afloat the next morning. The captain and a salvage crew returned to put out fires, reduce the list, and bury the dead, including Red.

Yorktown was taken under tow by a fleet tug on a course for Pearl Harbor. A Japanese submarine discovered the slow-moving carrier, and fired two torpedoes into her port side. Battle flags still flying, *Yorktown* survived another night, then she sank sixteen thousand feet to the bottom of the Pacific and settled upright in the cold darkness.

The Japanese lost all four carriers and twice as many planes as the Americans at Midway. The tide of the Pacific war had turned.

Chapter 13

Mark's parents had a long talk with him about death that he refused to hear. Man-is-born-and-he-dies-stuff. Ashes-to-ashes-and-dust-to-dust-stuff. Red-is-dead-but-we-should-be-happy-he's-in-heaven-stuff.

Mark slept so deep to blot out the pain that waking was like a struggle back to life. It was the beginning of healing.

Swede and Red were never close. Swede saw Red's death in terms of his own impending military service. Red was a hero. It might be worth dying to be remembered that way. Swede used school as an excuse to miss the memorial service.

St. Mary's was packed. The Aces and their families took up five pews. Mark sat between Clancy and his wife. Dan Lee's wreath dominated the sanctuary, a five-foot baseball diamond of green and white carnations with a broken heart of red roses at second base.

Father Sears leaned on the pulpit and said some prayers for Red, told what a fine man he was and how he'd be missed. The old priest wiped away tears with a handkerchief he kept stuffed up his cassock sleeve.

Frank Collins delivered a brief eulogy. He had Red's hair and freckles, but was half-a-head taller and fifty pounds heavier.

"Red was my big brother," Frank said. "He taught me everything that was important when we were growing up, how to farm, hunt, fish, and throw a curve ball." He nodded to himself several times.

"Red enlisted in the Navy the first time when he was seventeen. Some of you know that if it hadn't been for his financial and moral support, I'd never have been able to attend college and get my teaching degree. He sacrificed for me..." Frank gestured toward the front pew. "...and my wife Mary and daughters Ellie and Margie.

"Red always said that my family made him proud, and we loved him for that; but Red had so much to be proud of himself..." Frank cleared his throat.

"Red played for the Chicago Cubs. He was so shy that nobody would have known it, except that the *Courier* used to run a special column telling what he'd done in spring training, the regular season, and the '35 World Series. It was called 'The Red Collins Recap.' Remember?"

There were murmurs of recognition in the congregation.

"In closing, I'm going to tell you something not many people know. Red could have had a military deferment because of his baseball injuries. He could have stayed home, run the farm, played for the Aces—but Red wanted to serve his country. God bless you, Red. Rest in peace."

The only sounds in the church were mourners' crying and coughing. Mark skipped the luncheon in the church hall, and took his grief to the solitude of the treehouse.

There was a sense of incompleteness without a burial service, but Red's funeral rites had been conducted by *Yorktown's* captain on the ship's hanger deck on the morning of June 6. After brief prayers, Red and the last of his dead shipmates were slipped over the side with five-inch shells tied to their ankles to make sure they sank.

MARK PENN GOES TO WAR

Red's death gave Mark second thoughts about Cathy. His moping for her mocked his sorrow for Red. Cathy had been a comet blazing through his life, then gone. Red was the north star, constant and reassuring.

Still, Cathy wouldn't go away. Every time Mark went to the mailbox, he expected a letter from her. Two days after the memorial service, there was a letter for Mark; but it wasn't from Cathy, it was from Red.

His first thought was a wild prayer that Red was still alive, even though he knew it couldn't be true. The letter was dated May 30, 1942, the day *Yorktown* left Pearl Harbor for the Battle of Midway. Mark's hands shook as he read:

Hi Pal,

Wish I could tell you where I've been and where I'm going, but I'm sure you understand why I can't. Come to think of it, I don't have the slightest idea where I'm going.

This was always my favorite time back home with planting done and everything sprouting. Then I remember that I'm not a farmer anymore. I miss it though. What I miss even more is playing ball. Hope the team is winning, and I have a year or two left in me after the war. Say hello to Clancy and the guys. Keep second base warm for me.

I understand how you feel about not being old enough to join the Marines. You'd be a good one. Your time will come soon enough. Just keep your chin up, and say a prayer for me. I know that with guys like you putting in a good word with the Lord,

⮑ 59 ⮐

things will be okay.

Tell your mom thanks for the cookies. She's a good cook.

I have to go on watch now. Keep those letters coming. They mean more than you can imagine.

Your friend,
Red

Chapter 14

Mark sleep-walked through the next week—the Fourth of July parade and fireworks, the Aces' 6 to 2 win over Faribault, and the start of dog days. Swede was seeing Jane every day after school. Mark sometimes joined them for Cokes at the Candy Shoppe, but his heart wasn't in it. His heart wasn't in anything.

Mark was biking past the Municipal Building one morning when he spotted a gold star next to Red's name on the Roll of Honor. Tears blinded him for a moment, then he wiped his eyes on his shirt sleeve, gritted his teeth, and vowed never to break down in public again. Sure, his old pal was dead, but bawling like a baby wasn't the answer.

He already knew the answer. It had been budding in his brain all week. Red had been killed by the Japanese. There were Japanese on the ridge. He'd go back and find out who they really were. It was the least he could do for Red.

Mark followed the creek up the ridge, tense with caution, eyes everywhere. He stopped behind the maple. Ann Matsui was sitting cross-legged in the grass by the garden humming to herself. The Doberman dozed by her side.

The dog's ears went up, his eyes opened, and he charged at Mark with high-pitched barks.

MICHAEL SPRINGER

Ann got to her feet. "Who's there?"

Mark eased sideways from behind the tree. The dog stood rigid, teeth-bared.

"Brutus, come here," she said.

The Doberman gave Mark's pantleg a sniff, and scampered to Ann's side.

"Will he bite?" Mark said as he edged toward her.

"If he thinks you taste good. What're you doing here?" She stared at him.

"I just thought I'd...come and see you."

"Aren't you afraid my father will chop your head off?"

Mark flinched. "I had a dog. His name was Wink. He was hit by a car. Killed. I miss him."

She nodded and scratched the dog's ear. "I'd miss Brutus, too. He hasn't been in a very good mood lately. We had burglars awhile back."

"You did?"

"Yes, but they got away. Two of them."

"Did you call the police?"

"No, my father hopes to catch them himself. They left a clue behind."

"Clue?" Mark racked his brain for anything the boys might have forgotten. "What kind of clue?"

"Oh, I can't tell you that." She placed a finger to her lips. "It's a secret."

Mark glanced around. "Where's your father now?"

"He and my mother are visiting relatives for a few days."

"You have relatives nearby?"

She nodded.

That was bad news. There might be a whole network of Japanese spies. "So, you're all alone then."

"Why shouldn't I be alone. I'm almost thirteen. Besides, I have Brutus."

"Brutus. You think he'd mind if I petted him?"

"Ask him."

Mark squatted. Freedom of movement depended on having the dog's confidence. "You mind, Brutus?" He rubbed the dog's ears with both hands, and the Doberman's eyes closed in gratitude.

Ann gave Mark a little shove. "What're you really doing up here?"

"What d'ya mean?" Mark stood up.

"How come you're so friendly? Most of the people we've met since the war have been mean."

"Well, you can't blame them much, not after Pearl Harbor."

"I didn't bomb Pearl Harbor."

"The Japanese did, and you're Japanese. My best friend was killed on the *Yorktown*. The Japanese killed him."

"I'm sorry for your friend, but I'm an American." Tears glazed her eyes.

"What's that supposed to mean?"

"I was born in California, and that means I'm just as much an American as you are." She brushed the tears away with her hand.

Mark knew from civics class that if this girl really had been born in California, she was an American citizen. "What about your folks?" he said.

"They were born in California, too. So was my brother, John."

"Where's he?"

"Locked up at the Fort Lincoln internment camp in North Dakota. John would have been safe if he'd come to Minnesota with us, but he stayed behind with a friend. They were arrested on their way east."

"Why?"

"Nobody would sell them food or gas because they were Japanese-Americans. The police threw them in jail like they were tramps, and the FBI sent them to Fort Lincoln like they were spies or something."

"Well, it's hard to tell who's a spy these days."

"Maybe you think I'm a spy. Or my father." Ann glared at Mark.

"I..."

"You're just like the rest. It makes me wonder if all the things I learned in school about liberty and justice were just words."

"I didn't mean..."

"My father's family in Japan were samurai, a class of great warriors you can't even imagine. And people here treat him like dirt. In the last war, he was a lieutenant in the Army infantry—the United States Army. He was wounded in France. That's why he limps. He was awarded the Silver Star for bravery by General Pershing personally. And you talk of spies. You make me sick."

Brutus growled. Mark was silent. He'd already said too much if he intended to get on her good side.

"I'm sorry if I hurt your feelings," Mark finally said.

"I don't have feelings anymore. You'd better go."

"Do you mind if I come back again, maybe tomorrow?"

"You'd better watch out or people will say you're friendly with spies. Or maybe you're the spy, sneaking around, hiding behind trees."

Mark put his fists on his hips. "You complain about people being mean, but when I try to be friendly, you get mean. Maybe that's why people are mean, and not because you're Japanese."

Ann stuck out her jaw, turned, and walked toward the house. Brutus followed.

"I'll see you tomorrow," Mark said. "Same time, same place. Okay?"

She spoke over her shoulder. "I wouldn't. You might lose your head."

Mark watched as Ann disappeared around the back of the house. Maybe her father had been a hero in the Great War, but the enemy then was Germany, not Japan. She said he was a lieutenant, but the uniform in the cellar was a sergeant's. And there was no Silver Star ribbon on the jacket. Mark didn't know what to believe.

What was the clue her father had found in the cellar? That could mean trouble. Swede should know about this, but he'd hold off telling his pal until he had more evidence.

He'd come back tomorrow to get that evidence. This time Mark would control his emotions and try extra hard to become friends with her. She was pretty. Mark was already looking forward to seeing her again.

Ann watched from the kitchen window as Mark walked into the woods. His attitude toward her was unforgivable. Still, she hoped he did come back tomorrow.

Chapter 15

Mark returned to the Matsui property the next morning, eager but cautious. The Ford was still gone. Ann was hoeing in the garden. She glanced at him as he edged around the maple, but kept working. Brutus lumbered up to Mark, accepted several pats on his bony head, and went back to the shade of the front steps.

"Good morning," Mark said. He sat beside Brutus.

Ann wiped her brow on her sleeve, and leaned on the hoe. "Just what does a batboy do?"

"Come to practice Wednesday, and I'll show you."

"Last time I went anywhere, a boy slugged me."

"Where? California?"

She nodded. "Spit on me, too."

"What? Nobody'd do anything like that while I was around."

She closed one eye and stared at him with the other. "What would you do, Sir Galahad?"

Mark shrugged. "I'm tougher than I look."

"If you really want to do something tough, grab the other hoe on the back porch and help me."

"It's too hot to work. Anyway, I've got my own garden to weed. Let's have a swim in the river instead."

"You don't want to swim with a spy."

"Come on, don't talk like that. I've got a treehouse right on the river." He pointed.

"It's too dangerous."

"The river's shallow this time of year. Besides, there's a backwater off the main channel we use."

"Who's we?"

"My pal, Swede Larson and me."

"What would he think of my being there?"

"He's in summer school every morning. He flunked geography."

Ann's eyebrows went up. "I don't have a suit."

"We can swim in our underwear."

"I don't trust you."

"I wouldn't do anything, honest." He crossed his heart.

"I don't mean that. Yesterday you were mean, today you're nice. How come?"

"I want to be friends."

"With a Japanese?"

Mark eyed her. "Friendship works both ways."

She cocked her head and thought for a moment. "Okay."

Ann lay the hoe against the scarecrow, locked Brutus behind the fence, and walked into the woods with Mark.

"I've been meaning to ask," he said. "What's that fish hanging from the flag pole holder by the front door?"

"It's called a balloon carp. May fifth in Japan is the Boys' Festival. Families hang one carp for each boy, usually from a long bamboo pole on the ground or roof. Carp for older boys can be twenty-feet long. Younger boys have smaller ones. The air fills them and they look like they're swimming."

"It's not May now."

"My father is flying the carp for my brother till he comes home."

Ann and Mark crossed the railroad tracks and Bottom Road, then stumbled down the riverbank and stopped.

Mark looked up. "There's the treehouse. Swede and I built it. You can't tell anybody where it is."

"I won't." She raised her right hand.

"The river's down that path through the trees. Go behind those bushes and undress. I'll go in the water first. And watch out for poison ivy."

Mark undressed to his boxer shorts, raced to the water, and dove in. He kept his back to the shore until he heard a splash. A few minutes later, Ann dog-paddled to his side.

"Nice, huh?"

Ann smiled. "We used to swim in the Kern River in Bakersfield, but this is much greener, like the Garden of Eden."

He gestured toward midstream. "Race you to the sandbar. We call it the point. Okay?"

She nodded.

They stayed side-by-side for ten yards, then Mark pulled away. Nobody could out swim him, not even Swede.

Mark reached the point and turned to claim victory, but Ann was not behind him. She'd drifted into the main channel, where she was about to be swept downstream. The Minnesota looked slow and calm, but its currents and whirlpools could be deadly.

Mark yelled, "Come back."

Panic etched Ann's face and she began to thrash.

Mark swam to her side with all his strength. She flung her arms around his neck and they both went under. He grabbed Ann's hair and pulled her to the surface.

"Stop fighting me or we'll both drown," he shouted. "Stop it."

Ann went limp. Mark grabbed her around the waist and swam one-armed to the point. All the lessons he'd learned in life-saving class really worked.

Ann crawled onto the sandy beach and lay on her stomach. She was wearing a pink cotton union suit that was cut like a one-piece bathing suit. Mark placed a steadying hand on her bare back as she coughed and panted. Finally, she let out a big sigh and sat up.

"I should have warned you," Mark said, trying not to stare at the curve of her breasts.

"I should have been more careful. I'd better get dressed."

"I'll swim alongside, just in case."

Ann gave him a weak smile, and slipped into the water. She and Mark dog-paddled back to shore. They dressed in private and met under the rope ladder. Mark had hung his shorts to dry on the branch of a dwarf birch. Ann had made a small bundle of her wrung-out union suit.

"How do you get up there?" she said.

"It's easy. Watch."

Mark shinnied up the rope into the treehouse. Ann lobbed her underwear up to him. It took Ann three tries to make it into the treehouse, and then Mark had to give her a hand. She draped the union suit on the east window sill to dry. They sat cross-legged on opposite sides of the foot locker.

Ann arranged her hair with her fingers. Mark could see her entire face for the first time. She *was* pretty.

"Thank you for saving my life."

Mark smiled.

"It would have broken my parents' hearts. They have enough sorrow in their lives with my brother's troubles." She looked away for a moment. "I told you that they were visiting relatives. It isn't true. They've gone with a lawyer to see about getting John out of that awful camp."

"I hope they can."

"Really?"

"Sure. He didn't do anything wrong, did he?"

"No."

"Then he shouldn't be there."

Ann's eyes brightened. "When he comes home, you can meet him. John loves baseball as much as you do. He was the center fielder for the Bakersfield Braves last year and hit over .300. Maybe he could play for your team."

"Well, it isn't exactly my team."

"You could talk to somebody."

Mark shrugged. What would Clancy think if he showed up one day with John Matsui? Things were getting complicated.

Things got a hundred times more complicated when Swede's whistle cracked the silence. His big Keds were pounding down the river path.

Mark got to his knees. "That's Swede. If he finds you here, he'll kill me."

"Why?"

"Never mind. I'll go down and talk him into having a swim, then you take off."

"But I'm scared to go down alone."

"You'll be more scared if Swede finds you here. And get rid of this." He snatched Ann's union suit and tossed it in her lap.

Mark slid down the rope as Swede came charging up the path.

"How come you're not in school?" Mark said.

"I got kicked out for not doing my homework. I can't go back till I turn it in." He grabbed the rope.

"Where you going?"

"To get my smokes, then have a swim."

"Thought you quit smoking."

"I changed my mind." Swede squinted at Mark. "What's the matter? You look like you saw a ghost."

"Nothing's the matter. Let's have a swim first, then have a smoke."

Swede glanced up at the treehouse. "What's going on?"

"Nothing's going on. How come you're so suspicious?"

"Because you're acting funny." Swede let go of the rope. "Oh, no. You lost my telescope again."

"No, I didn't. I haven't used it since last time. Honest." Mark raised his right hand.

"You don't mind if I check?" Swede eyed him.

Mark sagged and spoke in a trembly voice, "If my word isn't good enough..."

A soft thump in the treehouse silenced Mark. The rope swayed.

Swede whispered, "Somebody's up there."

Swede shinnied up the rope until his head cleared the trap door, then he twisted himself in a slow circle and crawled inside.

"Nobody here," Swede yelled down to Mark.

Mark climbed the rope and crept to Swede's side. He surveyed the treehouse, corner-to-corner, floor-to-ceiling. Where had Ann gone?

Swede checked the safe and smiled when he found his telescope. He tapped Mark on the shoulder. "Sorry, I was just PO'd about getting kicked out of class." He took a crumbled pack of Camels out of the foot locker and lit up.

"You been spying on the Japanese?" Swede said.

"Naw. I went up the other day, but nobody was around. I'll bet they moved away."

"Good riddance to bad rubbish. Come on, let's have a swim. I'm roasting."

The boys undressed in the treehouse, then went to the river for a long swim. Mark kept an eye on the area around the black oak, but didn't see Ann. When they returned to the treehouse, Mark went up first, just in case.

It was a good thing he did because Ann's underwear was hanging in the east window. Mark just managed to throw it outside before Swede came through the trap door.

That Ann Matsui was dangerous.

Chapter 16

Mark needed Swede in school every morning if he was to advance his friendship with Ann and find out more about her family. That meant helping Swede do the homework he'd skipped, writing out a list of South American rivers: the Amazon, Orinoco, La Plata, and all the rest. Mark knew them by heart because he loved learning about other nations. Swede still thought that geography was a waste of time. Who cared what the capital of British Guiana was?

The moment Dorothy Penn left for her Red Cross class the next morning, Mark headed up the ridge. He studied the Matsui property from the maple. The Ford was still gone. Ann was playing jacks on the front stoop.

Brutus spotted Mark from the shade of the steps, ambled to his side, and rubbed against his pantleg. Mark gave the Doberman's neck and ears a long scratch, then walked toward the house.

Ann didn't look up when Mark passed through the gate and clopped up the walk. He pulled her underwear out of his back pocket and dropped it on her jacks.

Ann tossed the underwear aside and continued the game, bouncing a little red ball and scooping up the aluminum jacks. She was good at it.

"Is your friend with you?" she finally said.

"I told you, he's in summer school."

"Good riddance to bad rubbish."

Mark had a sinking feeling. "Where were you?"

"Outside that window." She looked up at Mark. "Hanging by my fingernails."

"While we undressed?"

Ann giggled.

Mark's bad temper was rising. "You know, you almost got me in a lot of trouble with Swede, and after what I did for you."

Ann gave him a hard look. "Did you call the paper and radio station to tell them what a hero you were?"

"I didn't mean that. Why do you have to be such a smart aleck? I've been trying to be friends, but I guess you don't want to be. Right from the start you've been this way. You said your father was a chick sexer. I looked it up at the library and asked around, but nobody ever heard of it. And you act like I'm stupid because I don't know what it means."

"I told you what it means."

"That doesn't mean I understand it."

Ann made a sack out of her underwear, put the ball and jacks inside, and stood up. "Do you like tea?"

"Tea?" What was she up to now?

"I usually make tea every morning about now. Would you like some?"

Mark shrugged. Here was a chance to get inside again. "Sure."

"You have to take off your shoes. Leave them inside."

Ann opened the front door and they entered an enclosed porch. Mark took off his tennies. Ann kicked off her zoris and eased into a pair of green, backless slippers. Mark put on a matching pair, and shuffled after her through a second door into the kitchen with its sink and pump, pantry, wood stove, door to a back porch and cellar steps, stairs to the second floor, round oak table with four matching chairs.

Ann led Mark through a door on the right into the parlor, except that no Minnesota parlor ever looked like this one.

The floor was covered with tatami, straw mats bound with string and edged in black linen. The smell reminded Mark of his grandpa's hayloft.

On the far wall was a kakemono, a hanging picture of a cherry tree in full bloom. Below on the floor was a bonsai, a miniature live pine in a pale-green porcelain pot. In the center of the room was a low rosewood table and a pile of five zabutons, saffron-colored pillows.

Ann gestured with her hand. "This is a Japanese-style room where we spend a lot of our time. In Japan, families would sleep and cook here, too, but we have upstairs bedrooms and the kitchen just as we did in Bakersfield."

"If you're really Americans, why do you live this way?" Mark said.

"We don't have much choice now. Our trailer is small, so we could only take the things that meant the most to us. Most were inherited from Grandfather Matsui."

"What happened to the rest of your stuff?"

"We sold our house and most furnishings in a hurry at a loss because my father had heard rumors about the camps, and wanted to leave for Minnesota. Friends and neighbors who had nowhere to go lost even more when they were forced to sell on short notice. My father calls the people who cheated us vultures."

"It's not right," Mark said.

"No." Ann took one of the pillows and placed it by the table. "You sit here with your back to the takonoma in the place of honor."

Mark thought he'd rather face the display on the far wall, but Japanese obviously had different customs. He sat on the plump pillow and crossed his legs under the table.

"I'll make the tea and be right back. You sit tight." Ann smiled and left the room, closing the door behind her.

Mark waited a moment, then went to the door and listened to Ann pump water into a tea kettle. He had time to look around before the water boiled.

There was a closet on an inside wall. Mark opened the door. A single wire hanger dangled from a pipe rack. A high shelf looked empty. Mark did a little jump to check. There was a shoe box all the way back. He used the hanger to pull the box into his hands.

The box contained an unloaded Luger and full magazine with eight 9mm rounds. It had to be the pistol that bushy-faced guy gave Matsui. Mark sniffed the gun. A smell of oil, not gunpowder, meant that it hadn't been fired recently. Red had taught Mark about firearms and their safe use. Why did the old man keep the Luger here where the family gathered? Did that mean Ann and her mother knew about it?

Mark replaced the pistol, shoved the box to the back of the shelf, and closed the closet door. He went to the draped window and peeked out.

Standing in the woods near the maple was Chief Morton in civilian clothes. With him was a tall, slim man in a dark suit and hat. There was no car in the driveway. Where'd they come from?

When Mark looked back, the men were gone.

The man with Morton was FBI agent Ted Cole, who'd driven

from Minneapolis for the day. Aware that the Becks were working at the Colt factory and the Matsuis were in North Dakota, the men had decided to reconnoiter the two properties. They were planning a showdown they hoped would close "The Nisei Case."

Chapter 17

Mark heard Ann's hand on the doorknob, and dashed back to his place at the table. She entered the room carrying a red and black lacquer tray that held six pieces of Satsuma porcelain: a squat tea pot with curved handle and spout; two cups and saucers; and a covered bowl. She told him that the richly colored ceramic ware had been in the Matsui family for a hundred years. Ann would be in trouble if anything happened to it, but she felt a powerful need to show Mark that the real Japan was more about beauty than bombs.

In one graceful move, Ann sat Japanese-style on the back of her legs, and placed the tray on the table. She half-filled a cup with steaming tea, and placed it in front of Mark.

He hesitated. This tea was green, not dark-orange like his mom's. The cups didn't have handles. And where were the cream and sugar?

Ann poured herself some tea, then uncovered the bowl. "Have some cakes."

The cakes were like sugar cookies. Mark took one, nibbled on it, and popped the rest in his mouth.

Ann sipped her tea with both hands, and Mark did the same. It was hot. And strong. Mark's eyes watered. In no time, they finished off the cakes and were on their second cup of tea.

Mark felt guilty about enjoying himself with something so Japanese. Swede would never believe it.

Mark didn't know that the traditional tea ceremony, which Rose Matsui had taught her daughter, was long, formal, and complicated. Ann had made this Nihon-cha the quick, modern way—used even in Japan—by pouring boiling water over tea leaves in the pot.

When they'd finished, Ann put the chinaware on the tray, and turned to Mark. "I want to explain about my father's work. I know it can be hard to understand."

"That's for sure."

"It's really very special. Only a few hundred in the whole country can do it, and most are of Japanese descent. It's important to the war effort, too."

"How?"

"His job is to inspect the newly hatched chicks and separate the females from the males. Since the females lay eggs, they're more valuable."

Mark wasn't sure he agreed with that. "What happens to the males then?"

Ann hesitated. "They kill them."

"Kill them. What for?"

"Because it costs more to feed them than they're worth."

"How does that help the war effort?"

"It's important that the chicken and egg industry be efficient. No feed is wasted on chicks that can't lay eggs."

"What's so hard about telling chickens apart anyway? Roosters are easy to spot."

"But these are chicks. They all look alike, don't they?"

Mark nodded. He remembered the flocks of yellow "peeps" in

the brood house on his grandpa's farm. "How does he tell the difference?"

"He turns them upside down under a bright light. Only experts can do it. My father can sort a thousand chicks an hour."

"I don't see why they have to kill the males." Mark bowed his head.

"I don't either, but that's the way they do things." Ann touched his arm. "Maybe I shouldn't have told you."

Mark shrugged. "I'm glad I'm not a chick."

"Me, too." She smiled. "You said you wanted to be friends. So do I."

Ann's face was so close, Mark could smell her sweet breath. He had a strong urge to kiss her.

"I cut out the article about you in the paper. It said you were twelve and went to Middleton Public. That means we'll be in the same grade this fall."

Mark pulled back. "You're going to go to school here?"

"I have to go somewhere. It'll be nice to have someone I know in my class."

Mark gave her a thin smile. He foresaw big problems being friends with the only Japanese in the school. "You didn't come to school after you moved here," he said. "Where did you go?"

"My mother tutored me. She was a teacher before she met my father."

"Do you go to church in town?"

"My father talked to some pastors, but they didn't think we should attend services, for our own safety."

Mark frowned. "Don't you go anywhere? The movies?"

"We don't go out in public much to avoid...problems. There's another Japanese family in St. Peter, the Yamaguchis. Mr. Yamaguchi works with Father at the hatchery. Last time we visited them, one of their neighbors called the police."

"What for?" Mark said.

"They thought we were spies or something, but we were only playing Monopoly." Ann gave Mark a sad look and stood up. "I have to weed and do some other chores. Can you come back tomorrow? I'll make tea again."

Mark agreed. They went to the front porch, put on their shoes, and walked toward the garden. Brutus got up, stretched, and sauntered after them.

Mark noticed the Beck mausoleum in the woods and pointed. "What's that little building way back in there?"

"I heard that one of our neighbors' ancestors was a stone mason, and he built it for his wife's grave—like the Taj Mahal. It's haunted."

"What d'ya mean?"

"I've seen strange things out there at night from my bedroom. Lights and shadows and noises." Her eyebrows went up. "Ghosts, maybe."

"There's no such thing as ghosts."

"Something."

Mark decided to steer clear of that graveyard from now on.

They said goodbye at the edge of the garden. Mark scratched Brutus's neck, and headed down the ridge. The Matsuis had been lucky to avoid an internment camp, but they were prisoners just the same. How could this happen in America? He must be the only friend Ann had. And nobody knew about it. Maybe that was for the best.

Ann took the hoe and weeded among the cabbage heads. Being Mark's friend wasn't going to be easy. He'd turned pale when she mentioned school. Nobody in Bakersfield stood up for her when classmates called her names and spit on her. If that happened here, would Mark take her side?

She leaned on the hoe and smiled. Yes, Mark was the kind of boy who'd be gallant. He was a straight-arrow, like John.

Chapter 18

The next morning after tea and cakes, Ann said, "I've got a surprise for you." She took a brass Radio Orphan Annie decoder badge out of her pants pocket. "Pretend it's a medal for saving my life." Then she pinned it to his shirt, and kissed him on both cheeks the way they did in the movies.

What happened next was an even bigger surprise, and something Mark would never forget. Ann led him by the hand through the kitchen to a small room off the back porch. There were built-in cabinets along the inside wall, and in the far corner was an unpainted wooden box four-feet-square and two-feet deep. Pine scent filled the air.

"This was an old laundry room," Ann said. "Our landlords helped my father turn it into a bathroom."

Mark pointed. "You mean that thing's a bathtub?"

"Not just any bathtub." Ann removed one of two slats from the top of the box. A whoosh of steam escaped. "It has a water heater. You want to take a bath?"

"You think I'm dirty or something?"

"This tub isn't for getting clean, it's for relaxing. You wash yourself outside the tub, then get in and soak." She smiled.

"Why didn't you put in an American bathroom when you remodeled, so you wouldn't have to go outside to the toilet?"

"The toilet and bathroom are separate in Japan. When my grandfather came to America, the thing he missed most was the o-furo, the bath. So he had one built. My father grew up loving the custom. So do I. You want to try it?"

"I don't know…" The tub reminded Mark of the watering trough in his grandpa's barnyard.

"Come on, I'll show you how. It's easy."

"You mean you'd be here while I did it?"

"I was going to take a bath with you. It's common in Japan."

"We're not in Japan now."

Ann sighed. "It's just a bath. We're not going to play doctor or anything."

Mark shook his head. "I don't think so."

"Okay. You'll never get a chance like this again."

Mark took a step forward, as if somebody had pushed him. Wasn't this something he'd been looking forward to all his life, even if he didn't know it?

"What do I do?" he said.

"First, take off your clothes and hang them in the closet over there." She removed the second tub slat.

"I'm not taking off my clothes unless you do."

"I'll be with you in a minute." Ann opened a wall cabinet and took out a round wooden bucket, a milking stool, a bar of soap, and two washcloths.

Mark kept his eyes on Ann as he undressed. The closet was like a cloakroom at school, only smaller. The hooks were nails. Swede had swiped his clothes once while he was swimming, and Mark had a fear of it happening again. She wouldn't do that, would she? He was down to his shorts.

"I'm not going any further till you take something off."

Ann gave him a sarcastic look, then in a flash removed her shirt and dungarees. She didn't have underwear on today.

Mark gaped at her nakedness. "Geez, you're all grown up."

"Don't you know it's not nice to stare. Come on, get undressed."

Ann dipped the bucket in the tub and poured water over her shoulders. She sat on the stool, soaked a washcloth in the bucket, and worked up a lather with the soap. Mark watched in fascination as she scrubbed herself all over, then rinsed off with water from the bucket.

Mark kicked his shorts into a corner of the closet, grabbed the bucket, and sidled to the tub with the bucket in front of him. He dipped the bucket into the water and poured a trickle over his shoulders.

"Yeow!" He dropped the bucket. "It's really hot."

"I hope you didn't crack the bucket." She picked it up and checked for damage.

Mark grabbed the bucket out of her hands, refilled it, and poured water over his shoulders. It didn't seem as hot this time. Then he sat on the stool, scrubbed himself with his soapy washcloth, and rinsed off.

When he turned, Ann was in the tub, up to her neck in the water. Mark stuck a toe in next to her.

Ann giggled. "You look like a ballet dancer."

She was staring right at him, but he couldn't just plunge into the tub. He'd be boiled like a lobster. Mark took his time and lowered himself in slow motion. Let her look. He finally settled on the rough bottom with his knees up and the water lapping at his chin.

Mark felt his body sag into total relaxation. He closed his eyes and leaned toward Ann until their shoulders touched. When she didn't move away, he opened one eye. Her eyes were shut tight, and she wore an angelic smile. Mark puckered his lips several times as he thought about kissing Ann and telling her he loved her. How could she look so calm?

Over the next few minutes, Mark accidently-on-purpose brushed her with his hip, arm, leg, and foot. It was all he could do not to touch her with his hands.

Brutus barked outside. Ann stiffened, then stood up. "They're home."

Her parents were back. Mark stood up.

"Quick," she said, "get your clothes and go out that door." She pointed. "Cut to the right and you'll be in the woods before they see you. I hope."

Ann leaped out of the tub, pulled a large towel from the cabinet, and began to dry herself off.

Mark splashed out of the tub and headed for the closet. He pulled on his dungarees and used his shirt as a makeshift knapsack for the rest of his clothes.

"My tennies," he said. "They're on the porch."

"I'll hide them. You'll have to go barefoot. Hurry."

She hung up the towel, slipped into her dungarees and shirt, and left the room without another word.

Mark opened the door, streaked to the maple, and checked to see if anybody was following. Nobody. The Ford was in the shed. The Matsuis must be in the house.

He grinned as he put on his shirt and stuffed the rest of his clothes into his dungaree pockets. How many guys had ever done anything like he did today? Nobody in Middleton, that's for sure. Who knows what might have happened if Ann's folks hadn't come home? Mark started down the ridge thinking about next time.

The Matsuis were exhausted after their overnight drive from Fort Lincoln, but happy to see Ann. They both hugged her.

"What's the news, Papa?" Ann helped him off with his suit coat and draped it over the back of a kitchen chair.

Matsui shook his head. "Not good. The Justice Department is going to deport Ken Nomura to Japan as an undesirable alien, and John's case is bogged down in paperwork."

"What about the lawyer?" Ann said.

"He's doing his best. We may have to go back next week." He sighed.

Rose took her husband's arm. "You'll feel better after a bath."

Ann moved her parents toward the stairs to their bedroom. "You two get unpacked. I'll make sure everything is ready for you in the o-furo."

When Rose and Robert Matsui went to take their bath, there was no sign that anybody had been there before them.

Chapter 19

John Matsui knew he was risking imprisonment by staying behind to help Ken Nomura settle his affairs. Nomura was a teacher of Japanese language and literature at Bakersfield State College, where John was a freshman. Ken planned to take John to Middleton in his '36 Buick, then drive to Chicago, where he had relatives. It turned out that Nomura was in the greater danger.

Like most Japanese-Americans, Ken had problems selling his home because buyers knew he'd be leaving one way or another and offered him only a fraction of its value. He finally rented the furnished home to a colleague, Frank Morrel of the French Department.

Robert Matsui had given his son a map marked with the location of friends who would provide Ken and him with food and gas on their way east. The men also loaded the Buick with cans of gas and extra food. They ran out of food, gas, and friends near Huron, South Dakota, and were arrested for vagrancy.

A check with the Justice Department revealed that Nomura was a Kibei, an American-born Japanese who'd been educated in Japan at military school. Kibei were considered high security risks. The fact that Nomura had taught a Japanese language course was further evidence against him. John was presumed guilty by association.

The men were handcuffed and sent under guard on a bus with barred and blacked-out windows to Fort Lincoln, North Dakota. This internment camp was located along the Missouri River, south of Bismarck. It had double ten-foot cyclone fences topped with barbed wire, and thirty-foot watch towers manned by armed sentries. Inmates were German and Japanese aliens, and others considered security risks.

Ken's Buick was sold by the arresting deputy sheriff. His home and furnishings were sold by Frank Morrel when the French professor got his draft notice at the end of the spring semester. Nomura never received a penny.

John wrote to his father, who contacted the Justice Department. All of Matsui's efforts to free his son failed because the FBI had decided to use John as bait to force the father's cooperation. Three months had passed with no results, so Agent Cole asked for a meeting with Matsui in Chief Morton's office. Cole sat in Morton's chair, Matsui across from him.

"Mr. Matsui, how are things coming with that boy of yours?" Cole said.

"You know very well how things are coming. You promised to help me."

"These things take time, Mr. Matsui. War slows down the bureaucracy. But I have a plan."

Matsui frowned, unable to hide his skepticism. "What kind of plan?"

"I want you to step up your complaining to the Becks about the way your son is being treated. Say you're disgusted and want to get even. Lose your temper. Talk about breaking into that camp, or blowing up bridges and dams. Make them show their hand."

"Break into Fort Lincoln? You haven't seen that place."

"Neither have the Becks."

"What if they turn me in?"

Cole chuckled. "They won't." He handed Matsui a small piece of paper. "I have to get back to Minneapolis. Here's my office phone number. Call me collect. And you have Morton's number."

"What about John?"

"Your son will be freed once you do this. If the Becks don't bite, well, we'll think of something else."

"I have your word?"

Cole offered his hand and Matsui shook it.

Matsui would have done almost anything to free John. The constitutional rights of over a hundred-thousand Japanese-Americans had been trampled on in the name of national security. What if the Becks were innocent, too? Once the war was over, he'd take his family to Arkansas, where Rose's cousin Eddy owned a truck farm and was considered a good neighbor, not a potential traitor. So far. First, he had to figure out how to approach the Becks tomorrow on the way to work.

As it turned out, Joe Beck approached Matsui, who was sitting between the brothers in the Chevy truck. "You seem a little down, Bob. What's the matter?"

"It's John. They're never going to let him out of that concentration camp. He hasn't done anything wrong. I'd like to blow the place up."

"What would you use, cherry bombs?" Joe said with a wry smile.

"I don't know. This whole thing is driving me crazy. Rose, too. I swear, if I had a chance to get even, I would."

"Fred and I understand, but I wouldn't let others hear you talk that way. You might wind up in a camp yourself, and then what would your family do?"

"A man can be pushed just so far!"

When Fred changed the subject to the upcoming Aces' game against Owatonna, Matsui thought he'd failed, but that evening on the way home, Joe said, "Bob, you talked about blowing up that camp and maybe doing other similar things. Was it just talk or were you serious?"

"Dead serious. When the government treats loyal citizens like we've been treated, a person has the right to fight back."

Joe smiled and slapped the steering wheel. "I couldn't have said it better, my friend. Let us think about this, and we'll talk again, maybe after supper."

At seven, Joe phoned Matsui and asked him to meet the brothers at the mausoleum. The Becks were waiting when Matsui arrived.

Joe spoke in a quiet voice. "How do we know we can trust you?"

Matsui forced a smile. "I pay my rent on time."

"I think you know what Joe meant," Fred said, unsmiling. "You were saying things that could get you hanged or land you in prison for life."

"I feel backed into a corner," Matsui said. "They might never let John out."

Joe said, "If we take you into our confidence, we have to be sure of you."

"You can."

"What about your wife and daughter?" Fred said. "They could be in danger."

"From who?" Matsui crossed his arms to hold himself together.

Fred shrugged. "Enemies. Now, are you still serious about getting even?"

Matsui nodded. He hadn't considered that Rose and Ann might be pawns, too.

"We have plans," Fred said. "Big plans, and could use your help."

"What kind of plans?"

Joe smiled. "All in good time. We'll tell you when we're ready to move, and we expect you to be ready to go when we say so. Okay?"

Matsui nodded. "I'll be ready."

The Becks shook hands with Matsui, then headed home.

Matsui waited a few moments, then went to his cellar and phoned Agent Cole.

"It's a good start," Cole said, "but we need something more definite. The minute they tell you what they're up to, we'll move in. I'll alert Fort Lincoln, too, just in case they're crazy enough to try something there."

"You might start processing John's papers at the same time."

"I will, but we expect you to keep after them."

"They're cagey."

"We'll be cagier. Good work."

The men said goodbye and hung up.

Matsui sat in his desk chair and rubbed his thigh. This was worse than combat because he was risking his life for his family as well as his country. America had betrayed him, but nothing could make him betray America.

Chapter 20

Mark and Swede hadn't seen each other all week except at Aces' practice. Mark assumed it was because he'd been busy with Ann and Swede was busy with Jane, but there was a more troubling reason. Ernestine Larson had been in and out of bed all week with what she dismissed as a touch of the flu. When Swede urged her to see a doctor, she refused. Doctors cost money.

Swede had just returned home from his Saturday-morning geography field trip to the Middleton Stone Company, where workers were quarrying the same yellow limestone used in the Beck mausoleum. He went to his ma's bedroom, and sat on the edge of her bed.

Mrs. Larson opened her eyes. Her smile was full of love. "Hello, Sonny. I made some hot dish. It's in the oven."

"You shouldn't be out of bed, Ma. And don't call me Sonny."

"You'll always be Sonny to me. How was your bus trip?"

"Some guys sawing rocks. Who needs it?"

"You need it. I want you to get an education."

"And I want to join the Marines. I can go without your okay."

"And leave me alone? You wouldn't do that."

Swede sighed and stood up. "I'm going swimming."

"Have your lunch first. And wait an hour." Mrs. Larson closed her eyes.

Swede leaned down and kissed his ma's cheek. "If you aren't better by Monday, I'm calling a doctor."

Swede was near tears as he picked at his hot dish. Maybe he could talk to Doc Neal. Naw, all his patients were babies. Mrs. Penn might help. The women had become friends at Red Cross. Something had to be done.

After lunch, Swede peeked in on his sleeping Ma, then biked toward the river. Mark was weeding his garden, a fate worse than death. Swede whistled and pointed toward the treehouse as he whizzed by. Mark gave him the thumbs up.

Swede dumped his bike in the ditch, and was skidding down the riverbank when he caught a glimpse through the trees of somebody climbing the treehouse rope.

He stopped and yelled, "Hey, get the hell down from there!"

The intruder hit the ground running, and disappeared up the ridge. It was a kid. He wore a blue shirt, dungarees, and work shoes. Swede started after him, but didn't get close enough to see his face.

When Mark showed up at the treehouse a few minutes later, Swede told him what had happened.

Mark kept a cool head. "Anything missing?" He checked the safe. "Telescope's here."

"I caught him going up. If that kid spreads the word, everybody and his brother will be out here." Swede shook his big fist at the ceiling.

Mark was puzzled. What was Ann doing at the treehouse? Then his heart gave a little jump. Maybe she just wanted to say hello, the way he wanted to say hello to her. Maybe she just missed him, the way he missed her.

The first free time he had to go back on the ridge was Monday. He'd have to be careful now that her folks were back. Mark wasn't sure he could wait that long.

Chapter 21

The Aces extended their winning streak to four games Sunday in Owatonna as Doc Neal shut out the Hawks, 1-0. Allie New had the game winning homer in the sixth inning.

Swede usually met the team bus at Aces Park after road games, but he wasn't there today. Mark helped Albert unload equipment, then biked the two blocks to the Larson house. Swede looked glum when he answered the door.

"Where you been?" Mark said.

"My ma's in the hospital. Your ma talked her into going."

"She okay?"

Swede shrugged. "They stuck her with needles, took half her blood. I hate hospitals."

"It'll be okay, Swede. They'll find out what's wrong and fix her up."

"They better." Swede frowned. "I'm going to the hospital after school till they let her out. See you."

Swede shut the door so Mark wouldn't see him bawl. What would he do if anything happened to his ma? If it was up to Chief Morton, he'd go to Boys Town or reform school. For the first time in his life, Swede was scared.

Mark was dressing in his room the next morning when his mom

called upstairs to him. "Bring the dirty laundry in the hallway when you come down."

He gathered up the musty pile of clothing, towels, and wash-cloths. A sock dropped to the linoleum, then a small tan bag with a drawstring that'd be great for Swede's marbles. Mark stuck it in his back pocket.

Mrs. Penn was mixing a bowl of laundry starch on the kitchen counter. "Good morning, lazy bones. Teresa and Peter had break-fast an hour ago. Your oatmeal's on the table."

"I heard that Mrs. Larson's in the hospital. What's wrong with her?"

"They have to wait for the test results, but I don't think it's seri-ous."

"That's good. Swede's worried."

Mark dumped the laundry into a lined peach basket by the cel-lar door, and pulled the bag out of his pocket. "Where'd this come from?"

"I was going to ask you that. I found it in your dirty dungarees when I turned the pockets inside out last night."

"Mine?"

"Yes, yours. From now on, please empty out your pockets. And, for heaven's sake, why must you get your clothes so dirty? Now eat your oatmeal."

Mark had his breakfast, and escaped to the treehouse. He hung the bag by the drawstring on the corner of the open trap door where Swede would see it.

A plan had been squirming in Mark's brain all morning, and now it surfaced. He'd go on the ridge: first, to find out what hap-pened when Ann's folks got home; second, to see what she was doing at the treehouse when Swede almost caught her; and third, because he missed her.

"So what if I miss her?" Mark said aloud. "What's wrong with that? I like her. So what?" He glared at an imaginary audience for emphasis.

Mark charged up the ridge to the maple in what he figured was record time. Ann was hoeing in the garden. The Ford was in the shed, but nobody else was around.

"Psst!"

Ann looked to where Mark was hiding, and lay the hoe against the scarecrow. She wiped her hands on the sides of her dungarees as she walked to the maple. Brutus bounded after her.

Mark whispered, "Your folks home?" He ran his hands along the dog's sleek flank.

She nodded.

"Any trouble about my being here last time?"

She smiled and shook her head.

"What were you doing at the treehouse on Saturday?"

"I brought your tennies back, but I didn't have a chance to leave them."

"You shouldn't go without me. Swede was really mad, but at least he didn't recognize you."

"Sorry. I also went because I wanted to talk to you about John. They're letting him out of that camp. My mother and our lawyer left this morning to pick him up. I want you to meet him."

"What about your father?"

"Things will be fine when you help John play for your team."

Mr. Matsui's booming voice sounded from the woods. "I thought I told you to stay off my property."

Mark turned. Matsui was bearing down on him. He wanted to run, but his legs wouldn't move. Brutus slunk behind Ann.

Matsui stopped at Mark's side. "What're you doing here?"

"He came to see me, Father," Ann said.

Matsui turned to his daughter. "I warned you about such things."

"But he's my friend. His name is Mark Penn, and he said he'd help John play baseball for the Middleton team. Mark's the batboy." She smiled.

"Batboy? John won't have time for baseball." Matsui turned back to Mark. "I've a good mind to have you arrested for trespassing. I warned you once."

"Don't be angry with Mark," Ann said. "He saved my life."

"Saved your life? What're you talking about?"

Ann lowered her eyes. "I went swimming in the river one day when you and Mama were gone, and Mark saved me from drowning."

"You went swimming in the river?"

"I'm sorry for disobeying you."

"Get to the house."

Ann bowed her head, and scurried toward the house. Brutus limped after her.

"It's not her fault, Mr. Matsui," Mark said. "Swimming was my idea."

Matsui bared his teeth. "I'm not so angry that I can't thank you for saving my daughter's life. I'm going to let you go one more time, but if I ever see you around here again..." He clenched both fists.

Mark didn't stop running until he reached the treehouse. He climbed up the rope, sat in a corner, and hugged his knees until they stopped shaking.

He tensed at the pitter-patter of footsteps along the river path.

They were too light for Swede's. There was a tug on the rope. Mark crawled to the trap door. It was Ann. He slid down the rope.

"I thought you'd be in solitary confinement."

"My father had a meeting with our landlords. I hope they don't raise the rent. Anyway, I wanted to bring your tennies back." She took Mark's Keds out of her back pockets and gave them to him.

"Thanks." He lobbed them through the trap door into the tree-house.

"I don't think you should come back till I can tell him what kind of boy you really are. You may not believe this, but he's a very gentle man."

Mark turned up his nose.

"No, it's true. It's just since the war that he's turned bitter." She touched Mark's arm. "I'd better go. Don't forget about John. What if I leave you a note when he comes?" She looked around. "How about under that rock there?"

"Hide it good, so Swede doesn't find it. Maybe I can leave you a note, too, if something important comes up."

"Put it in the scarecrow's shirt pocket." She touched her breast.

"That's good. You could phone me if you want. The number's 2424. It's in the book under Thomas Penn, my dad."

"Our phone's broken. It's one of those old fashioned ones with a crank. What with the war, it'll take weeks to get it fixed."

"What about the one in the cellar?" Mark's hand went to his mouth.

"How do you know about the phone in the cellar?"

"I don't know. You must have told me about it."

"I didn't tell you about it. That phone is for my father alone."

Mark tried to smile, but it wouldn't come. "I confess, I went down in the cellar once when you were making tea or something."

Ann's expression turned hard. "You can't get to the cellar except through the kitchen, and that's where I make the tea."

"I went in from the outside." Mark felt the quicksand of his lies pulling him under.

"Those doors have been padlocked since the burglars…" Her eyes grew large. "You. It was you and your friend in the cellar that night. I should have known. You've been coming to see me all this time just to spy."

"Ann…" Mark put his hand on her arm.

"Don't." She jerked her arm away. "I hate you. You were lying to me right from the start." She began to cry.

"You lied to me, too."

Ann wiped her eyes on her sleeve. "When? Name one time I lied to you."

"You told me your father was a lieutenant in the Army. The uniform in the cellar was a sergeant's."

"So, you went through our things, too. My father received a battlefield commission. That was his old uniform. I've got a good mind to tell him."

"If you do, I'll tell him we took a bath together."

Ann's shoulders drooped. Her voice was cold. "I don't ever want to see you again." She turned and ran up the riverbank.

Mark stood trapped by his lies until the sounds of Ann's rushing through the underbrush were gone. It took an eternity to pull himself up the rope and into the treehouse. He collapsed beside his tennies.

Ann had replaced the broken and dirty laces with new ones. A Hershey kiss fell out of each shoe when he picked them up. Mark had never been so ashamed in his life.

Chapter 22

Mark was miserable. Ann's friendship had been sincere, his had been deceitful. He'd spit on her just as surely as those low-down kids in Bakersfield. The hurt in her eyes would haunt him forever.

That afternoon, he wrote a letter of apology to Ann. It took two hours and he wasn't satisfied with the results, but she had to know how sorry he was.

> Dear Ann,
>
> I've done some bad things in my life, but what I did to you was by far the worst. My heart hurts so bad, I can't stand it. I wish I was as big as Paul Bunyan. I'd use the sky as a blackboard and write I'M SORRY, ANN MATSUI for all the world to see.
>
> If you want to leave a note, put it under the rock by the treehouse. I'm sorry.
>
> Love,
> Mark

Mark debated using the word "love," but decided it would show sincerity. In any case, it was true, he did love Ann. Not the way he'd loved Cathy. That was baby love. His feelings for Ann were much more serious.

He went up on the ridge, and paused behind the maple. The Ford was gone. There was nobody around. Mark raced to the scarecrow, tucked the note into the shirt pocket, and dashed back to the maple. Still no sign of anybody. He went home feeling a little better.

Ann had been watching from the kitchen window, angry that Mark had disobeyed her father. Still, she was curious. When he was gone, she stole out to the scarecrow, plucked the note out of the pocket, and went to her room.

Tears poured down her cheeks as she read the note. Ridiculous tears. What was she crying about? That boy didn't deserve her tears. There were more important things to cry about. But the foolish tears just kept flowing.

Chapter 23

Mark didn't sleep well. He kept worrying about Ann's reaction to his note. The next morning when he checked the rock under the treehouse, there was no reply. Maybe she hadn't found his note. Maybe she had. She probably hadn't had time to answer. Ann would show up any second, and they'd be friends again. Mark waited, had a swim, read Swede's comic books, and felt sorry for himself.

The noon siren sounded. Swede would soon be at the treehouse. But his pal didn't show up. He must be with his ma. Or Jane.

Mark fidgeted awhile, then biked to town. He swung past the Larson house. Swede's Schwinn wasn't parked outside the back door, which meant he wasn't home.

By now, Mark was starved. He went home and made his favorite lunch: fried-egg sandwiches slathered with ketchup and milk black with Hershey's syrup. His mom would have a fit if she knew.

It was three by the time Mark got back to the treehouse. There was still no note from Ann and no sign of Swede. He hated days like this when nothing went right.

Mark nodded off, and was awakened by the whistle from the four-o'clock freight as it left the Middleton yard. Then he heard a slow, heavy clop along the river path. It sounded like Swede, but he

MICHAEL SPRINGER

always sprinted. Maybe it was Ann.

The treehouse rocked. Somebody was climbing the rope. Mark crawled to the trap door just as Swede poked his scowling face inside.

"What's the matter with you?" Mark said.

Swede sat hard beside him. "It's my ma. She's going to have a baby."

"Baby?"

"Yeah, it happened before my dad left, I guess. She's three months along. I didn't know old people did that kind of stuff."

"How come doctors didn't know sooner?" Mark said.

"The same stupid reason they didn't know Eva had diphtheria till it was too late."

"You always said you wanted another little sister. Maybe now you can have one, or a little brother."

"How would you like another sister or brother?"

"No thanks. How's your ma?"

"Home from the hospital, and happy as can be. I got the baby buggy down from the attic already." Swede shook his head.

"What'll your dad say?"

"She won't tell him right away, doesn't want him to come home and lose his job. Well, it could be worse. I thought she was dying."

Swede spotted the bag hanging from the corner of the trap door. "What's this?" He snatched the bag into his lap.

"Just a bag I found. I thought you could use it for your marbles."

"It's inside out." Swede righted the bag. "Hey, look at this!"

Stenciled in black letters on the side of the bag were the words, FIRST NATIONAL BANK OF MIDDLETON.

∽ 104 ∽

Swede waved the bag in front of Mark's face. "The *Courier* said that most of the cash taken in the Flag Day robbery was in bags like this. Where'd you get it?"

Mark told Swede what he knew about the bag.

"You mean you don't have any idea where it came from?"

"I never saw it before yesterday."

"Well, think." Swede tapped Mark's forehead with his index finger. "There's a thousand bucks reward."

A loud roar like thunder from downstream shook the treehouse. The bag flew out of Swede's hands, and he rolled onto his side. Mark grabbed the foot locker for balance.

Swede got to his hands and knees. "What the hell was that?"

Mark crawled to the north window. "Smoke out there."

Swede took his telescope from the safe. "Let's go look."

Mark grabbed the bag and stuffed it into his back pocket, then followed Swede through the trap door.

Chapter 24

Sirens and flashing red lights gained on Mark and Swede as they biked on the Bottom Road toward the shrinking gray smoke plume. The boys stopped on the shoulder to let two Middleton fire trucks pass. Right behind was Chief Morton's Plymouth. Seated beside him was FBI agent Ted Cole.

Three miles north of Sawmill Road, the boys slid their bikes into the ditch and joined the growing crowd. One nasty look from Morton sent Mark and Swede scrambling halfway up the ridge. They settled in the shade of a limestone outcropping, where they surveyed the chaos below with the telescope.

A massive landslide had blocked the Bottom Road. Forty feet of Chicago & St. Paul track had been blown up. The four-o'clock freight with seventy cars of war materiel sat just south of the explosion site. If it had been on time, the train and its five-man crew would have crashed into the river. Repairs would take two days.

Agent Cole pulled Morton away from onlookers. "This has to be what Matsui warned me about this noon."

Morton nodded. "If this really was the Becks' first move, then we'd better find out what else they've got in mind before somebody gets killed."

The Becks had approached Matsui as he ate his lunch on the

back dock of the Middleton Hatchery. The air was thick with the high-pitched peeps and fetid smell of newly hatched chicks. The brothers waved Matsui to the shade of a willow behind the plant. They sat in the silky summer grass. Matsui popped the last of a beef sandwich into his mouth.

"It's time," Joe said to Matsui with a cold stare. "We're ready to move. Are you still with us?"

Matsui swallowed hard and nodded. "What do I do?"

"Nothing for now," Joe said.

"We'll tell you what you need to know later. For now, just listen."

Matsui nodded. He had to remember everything for Agent Cole.

"Something has been set up," Fred said. "We aren't going to tell you what it is, but believe me you'll know when you hear about it." He smiled. "And soon."

"Think of it as a small sample of what's to come," Joe said.

"But why can't you tell me now?" Matsui said. "Don't you trust me?"

"Fred and I don't even trust each other." Joe winked at his brother.

Joe continued, "We want you to meet us at our house tonight at eight. We'll tell you then about the big plans we have. And I mean big. Beyond anything you can imagine." There was a wild look in his eyes.

"Eight o'clock," Fred said. "At our place. We'll leave the gate open."

The men got to their feet. The Becks shook hands with Matsui.

Matsui watched out of the corner of his eye on the way back to the plant as the brothers got into their truck and drove away. He hurried to the pay phone in the employees' locker room, called Cole collect, and told the agent what had happened.

"You think they meant today?" Cole said. "That doesn't give us much time."

"They just said soon."

"Then I figure if they're telling you tonight about future plans based on something already set up, it's got to be today. I'll drive down this afternoon with a couple of agents."

"To arrest them?"

"They haven't done anything yet, and I don't want to spook them. You have to consider that maybe what they told you was blarney to see what you'd do."

"They looked dead-serious to me."

"We'll soon find out," Cole said. "Now, here's the plan. You meet the Becks. My men and I will be nearby in case there's problems. If the meeting goes okay, call Chief Morton when you get back home and tell him what you've learned. We'll take it from there."

"What if something goes wrong?"

"We'll move in at the first sign of trouble. Maybe you'd better take that Luger along, just in case. You know how to use it?"

"Yes."

"And make sure your family keeps clear."

"I'm sending my daughter to St. Peter to stay with friends. My wife's on her way to Fort Lincoln with the lawyer to pick up my son. Thanks for that."

"Don't mention it. Good luck tonight."

The men said goodbye and hung up.

Cole hoped that Matsui could discover the Becks' plans, and save any showdown for a time and place of the FBI's choosing.

Cole and his agents arrived in Middleton at three-forty-five, thirty minutes before the explosion.

The bombing of the train tracks happened too late for the *Cou-*

rier's Tuesday edition. KMIN's *Six-O'clock News* reported that a landslide caused by recent heavy rains had buried the tracks. Authorities had clamped a blackout on the truth to avoid public panic and mislead the Becks.

The ruse didn't fool Mark or Swede. They were among the few who'd heard the explosion and connected it to the damage. The boys also knew that it hadn't rained in ten days. Something strange was going on. They wanted to know what it was.

Chapter 25

After supper, Mark and Swede took a roundabout way back to their limestone nook on the ridge because National Guardsmen were patrolling the area. Bulldozers had cleared the Bottom Road to traffic, and workers were laying new train track. Floodlights bathed the ridge in eerie shadows that had a hypnotic effect on the boys. Swede was soon snoring, and Mark was daydreaming about Ann.

She must have found his note by now. Why hadn't she answered it? He sure would like to take a bath with her again. It was the most exciting thing he'd ever done...

Mark jerked forward. His eyes sprang open. He shook Swede. "Hey, I think I know where I got the bag."

Swede was wide-awake. "Where?"

"Let me think a minute."

Mark steered his memory back to those panicky minutes after he left the Matsui bathtub and put on his pants. The bag must have been hanging on a nail in that closet or lying on the floor, and been scooped up with his socks and shorts. The problem was how to tell Swede without betraying Ann again. He'd have to stretch the truth a little.

Swede nudged Mark. "Well?"

"I've been going up on the ridge almost every day lately."

"So? What's that got to do with the bag?"

"That's where I found it, in the Matsui house."

"You were inside again?"

"Lots of times."

"How?"

"With Ann, the Japanese girl. That's her name, Ann." Mark smiled at the sound of her name.

"So you're old friends with her, huh?"

Mark shrugged.

"Where were her folks all this time?"

"Out of town."

"You do anything with her?"

"No, nothing like that."

"What then? What about the bag?" Swede edged closer.

"Well, you have to take your shoes and socks off when you go inside that house because that's the way Japanese do things. You put on these slippers."

"So?"

"The last time I was there, her folks came home."

"They did?" Swede grinned.

"Yeah. I didn't have time to put on my shoes or socks. It all happened so fast, but I think the bag was lying by my socks on the porch and I picked everything up together and stuffed them in my back pockets. Anyway, that's where my mom found the bag, in my back pocket."

"Pretty stupid, leaving the bag around like that. We have to tell somebody so we can get that reward. How about your old man?"

"He'd skin me alive if he knew I was at the Matsuis' house."

"He won't care about that once he sees the bag."

"Don't kid yourself. Besides, it'd get Ann in trouble."

"So what? Her old man has to be one of those robbers or he wouldn't have the bag. I'll bet he's a spy, too. Whose side are you on?"

"Ann knows we were in the cellar."

"How? You squealed."

"She wormed it out of me. Anyway, she said we left a clue."

"What clue?"

"She wouldn't tell me."

Swede sighed. "Well, it doesn't matter now. The important thing is to tell somebody about the bag, even if we do get in trouble."

"But who?"

The boys thought in silence for several minutes, then Swede elbowed Mark. "Somebody's coming up the ridge. Get down."

Mark and Swede hugged the ground. The crouched figure of Joe Beck moved through the dusky illumination from the floodlights and disappeared into the nightfall.

Mark whispered, "That was one of those guys who gave Matsui the Luger."

Swede slipped the telescope into a crevice and patted the flashlight in his back pocket. "Come on, let's see what he's up to."

Chapter 26

Joe Beck hurried along the top of the ridge toward the gate to his property. He'd skipped the eight-o'clock meeting with Matsui to see how the track repairs were coming. Trains would be running again by morning. All of that planning wasted. The timer had worked, but the freight was late. Next time they'd use a bomb that exploded on contact.

By now, Fred had met with Matsui and told him about their plans to dynamite the Colt .45 factory during dedication ceremonies Monday. Matsui wanted revenge and he'd get revenge. And this was just the beginning. There were hundreds of easy targets. Anything they could do to slow the American war effort would speed the fatherland's victory.

Mark and Swede watched from behind the DEAD END sign at the top of Sawmill Road as Beck entered the back porch of his house. The yard light went out.

Swede nudged Mark. "We could sneak up and look in the windows."

"I'm not taking any more chances."

The nine-o'clock curfew siren sounded at the fire station.

Mark said, "I have to get home. I'm late already."

"Let's check out the Japanese house, then go."

Swede turned on his flashlight and led the way through the woods. "Hey, there's that tomb. See any ghosts? Ohhhhh! Ohh-hhh!" He giggled.

"Knock it off, Swede. Somebody might hear you."

Swede stopped by the mausoleum door. He turned the knob and pushed with his shoulder. The door opened and a surprised Swede fell inside with a thud.

Mark knelt at Swede's side. "You okay?"

"Just a busted butt." Swede stood up and aimed his flashlight along the inside doorjamb. "Light switch." He clicked it on and closed the door.

Mark and Swede were blinded for a moment by the flash of fluorescent ceiling lights. The interior had been dug into the hillside and was four times as large as the exterior. The boys stared open-mouthed as they edged forward.

The room was paneled in knotty pine. On the far wall was a life-sized painting of Adolf Hitler. Another wall had framed war posters with German soldiers, tanks, and planes. A wooden rack displayed a dozen Mauser carbines. On the floor below was a crate of Lugers. A pile of Bund magazines sat on a workbench.

Swede picked up a magazine with a picture of Hitler on the cover, then flung it aside. "The Becks must be Nazis. Look at all this stuff."

Mark backed toward the door. "We'd better tell somebody."

One wall was lined with heavy shelves that held boxes with lumps of coal, silver pens and pencils, and sticks of dynamite.

Swede picked up a lump of coal and tossed it in his hand. "Hey, this isn't coal. Wonder what it is?"

"I don't know and I don't care," Mark said. "Let's go."

Swede put the coal back and headed toward the door. He paused at an oak armoire. The doors were open. Inside was a row of Bund uniforms, gray shirts and black trousers.

"What's this?" Swede reached inside the armoire and pulled out the limp legs of a Halloween skeleton costume. "Holy cats, let's get out of here!"

The boys rushed to the door, then stopped when they heard voices outside.

Swede flipped the light switch, and shoved Mark behind the armoire just as the door opened. The lights came on again. Joe Beck and Matsui entered the room.

Chapter 27

Matsui had never given the mausoleum more than passing notice. Burial grounds were sacred. But what was the FBI's excuse?

There were enough explosives in here to blow up all the rail lines, bridges, dams, and factories Fred had been itemizing for an hour. And Fred had bragged that he and Joe were the Victory Day robbers. All that cash meant for the war effort was being used to finance their traitorous plans. He had to get away and phone Chief Morton.

Joe took a silver fountain pen from a crate and held it up. "See this?"

"What is it?" Matsui said.

"Incendiary bomb. Toss it in a waste basket at the police station or armory and you've got the hottest fire you've ever seen." He put the pen back. "Sorry I wasn't at the meeting tonight. I haven't been in a very good mood since we missed bombing that train today."

Mark elbowed Swede. The Becks and Matsui had bombed the train tracks.

"I understand," Matsui said. "Just bad luck. I'm sure everything will be perfect when we bomb the Colt factory."

The boys turned to each other. Now those traitors were talking about the new Colt factory.

Beck checked his watch. "Except that I changed my mind. We're going to do it tonight. Fred should be along any minute."

"But why? Think of all the government officials and military brass you can eliminate at the dedication ceremony," Matsui said, trying to stall.

"Because I said so," Beck replied.

Swede shifted his feet to relieve the tension in his legs. The flashlight fell out of his back pocket and clunked to the floor.

Swede didn't hesitate. He put his hand on Mark's shoulder and whispered, "Stay put. One of us has to get away."

Both men were moving toward the noise. Beck had taken a Luger from under his belt. He slammed the armoire's doors shut. Swede stepped out to meet them.

"What the hell are you doing here?" Beck said.

Swede gave a little shrug that masked his fear.

"Get over there," Beck said, shoving Swede toward Matsui.

Beck craned his neck around the armoire, saw Mark cringing there, and yanked him out by the shirt sleeve.

Matsui's face was pale with surprise. "You."

"You know him?" Beck asked.

"He's been nosing around my place." Matsui pointed at Mark. "I warned you."

"What about the other one?"

Matsui shook his head.

Beck waved the Luger at the boys. "What're you doing here?"

Mark was so scared that he didn't know what to say even if he could talk.

Swede was scared, too, but he couldn't control his temper. "You damned Nazi. The cops know all about you. We saw you give this

Jap spy a Luger, and told Chief Morton..." Swede was having second thoughts, but it was too late.

Beck struck Swede across the face with the back of his free hand. Swede flew to the floor. Blood trickled from his nose. Mark was terrified that he was next.

Beck took a coil of rope from a workbench drawer and cut it into sections with a jackknife. He tied Swede's hands and feet, while Matsui did the same with Mark.

When they were done, Beck motioned Matsui away from where the boys lay. "If those two have been snooping around and saw us together, who knows what else they've seen and who they've told."

Matsui nodded. "What'll we do with them?"

"Why we kill them, of course."

"They're just kids." Matsui's knees were weak.

"And this is war. Besides, they've seen all this, and must have heard our plans for the Colt factory. We'll take them along and dispose of them there." Beck eyed Matsui. "You're not getting cold feet, my friend?"

"No, of course not."

"Good. Let's get Fred and load the truck."

As Matsui turned toward the door, Beck hit him on the back of the head with the Luger. Matsui groaned and crumpled to the floor.

Beck bent over Matsui. "I never did trust you, but you can still be useful."

He took a two-by-four inch-photograph out of his shirt pocket and slipped it into Matsui's shirt pocket. It was a reduced blueprint of the Colt factory with bomb locations marked.

"The government thinks your son is a spy. When the factory

goes up, they'll think you are, too."

Beck tied up Matsui, gave the Hitler portrait a stiff-armed Nazi salute, and strutted out of the mausoleum.

Mark shivered with relief, glad to be in one piece. He'd been unloosening the sloppy knots Matsui had tied. The old man would never make a Boy Scout.

"Swede."

"Yeah?"

"He's gone. You okay?"

"I guess so." He raised his bloody head. "Hope my nose isn't broken."

"I'm getting loose."

"Well, hurry up. You think Matsui is alive?"

"I don't know. He got hit pretty hard." Mark strained against his ropes.

"Serves him right," Swede said as he worked on his own knots.

Matsui moaned and his eyes blinked open. "What...what happened?"

Swede scooched toward him. "Your pal double-crossed you. How's it feel?"

Matsui jerked his blood-soaked head toward Mark. "I told you to keep away, but you wouldn't listen. Now you've ruined everything."

Mark freed his hands. "What're you talking about?" He began to untie his ankles.

"Never mind," Matsui said. "Just untie us, so we can get away. Hurry!"

"Nuts to you," Swede said. "You're in with the Becks. You helped rob the bank truck, plant bombs, and who knows what else?"

"No. They must have found out I'm working for the FBI."

"Then what about this?" Mark pulled the bank bag out of his back pocket and waved it at Matsui. "It's from the robbery. I found it in your house." Mark put the bag back in his pocket.

"Listen to me, batboy," Matsui said. "I never saw that bag before. I've been pretending to work with the Becks. I purposely left your knots loose so you could get away." Matsui sighed, lay his head on the cement floor, and passed out.

Mark sensed that there was truth in what Matsui said, but didn't have time to pin it down. He freed his ankles, got to his feet, and stumbled toward Swede.

A truck engine roared outside, then stopped. Doors slammed. Mark sagged.

"Hide somewhere," Swede said.

"Nowhere to hide." Mark tied a strip of rope around his ankles, curled up on the floor, and put his hands behind his back.

Joe and Fred Beck burst into the mausoleum. They dragged their captives outside by the feet and tossed them into the back of the truck. Mark was stunned, even though he was able to break his fall. Matsui wasn't moving. Neither was Swede.

Mark's fear had given way to lightheadedness. He had a plan. At the first chance, he'd leap off the truck and go for help. Nobody could catch him in the dark woods.

The Becks loaded the truck with crates of dynamite, caps, fuses, and timers. Joe turned off the mausoleum lights and locked the door with a key. He headed for the driver's door, Fred the passenger's door.

Mark got to his hands and knees, ready to escape once the truck started moving. But he'd already waited too long.

Chapter 28

It had been dark when Agent Cole and his two men left their unmarked black Ford on the Bottom Road and climbed the ridge. They'd settled in the woods along the weedy footpath between the Becks' and Matsuis' houses. Joe Beck had already returned home from the ridge, and the boys were in the mausoleum.

Now, Joe lit the way with a powerful flashlight as he and Matsui left the Becks' yard and walked along the path. Cole figured the men were going to Matsui's house, but they disappeared into the mausoleum. Cole had a glimpse inside when the lights went on, and saw the portrait of Hitler and shelves loaded with boxes. He was angry and embarrassed for all the times he and other agents had passed the mausoleum and failed to grasp its real function.

Cole resisted an impulse to raid the mausoleum. Fred was unaccounted for. Besides, he'd told Matsui that the FBI wouldn't act unless there was trouble.

The G-men waited as Joe went home and returned with Fred in the truck. The headlights were left on. Cole thought that maybe the brothers were going to move weapons or explosives. Instead, he watched as three bound bodies were thrown into the back of the truck. Cole assumed it was the Matsui family, and that they were dead. Why hadn't he acted sooner?

The Becks loaded crates of dynamite into the back of the truck. If gunfire hit those boxes, they might all be killed.

It was only when the Becks headed for the truck cab that Cole ordered his men into action. He shouted, "FBI. You're surrounded. Hands up."

The Becks went for their guns, and shot into the woods. Agents returned fire with their Thompson submachine guns, killing the Becks.

Mark had been peering over the truck railing when the shouting and shooting started. He dove for the truck bed and prayed. All the noise revived Swede.

Matsui was still unconscious when he was taken to St. Luke's Hospital by ambulance. Mark and Swede sat up front. The boys had told Cole most of what they knew, and been warned not to say a word to anybody about what happened.

The Becks' bodies were taken to the morgue by county coroner Earl Weber in his black Studebaker Express-Coupe. They'd be buried without ceremony two days later in their family cemetery.

Agent Cole supervised his men in inventorying the mausoleum's contents. They found forty thousand dollars in bank bags from the Victory Day robbery, plus a Midwest Bund membership list that was wired to FBI headquarters in Washington, D.C.

Mark and Swede slouched on a sofa in the hospital lobby waiting for Mr. and Mrs. Penn to pick up Mrs. Larson, then take the boys home. Their minor cuts and bruises had been treated. Swede was dozing. Mark was fidgeting, sure he'd be chained to his bed until school started in September for what he'd done tonight. He finally got up and wandered down the hallway and around a corner looking for a water fountain.

Ann Matsui slipped out of her father's room and spotted Mark down the hallway having a drink. "Psst!" She waved.

Mark wiped his mouth on his shirt sleeve, waved back, and headed her way.

Chief Morton had brought Ann to the hospital from the Yamaguchis' in St. Peter, revealed her father's undercover role, and sworn her to secrecy. Matsui had two broken ribs and a fractured skull, but was conscious. His wife and son John would be home tomorrow.

When Mark reached Ann's side, she saw the gash on his arm that had been painted with Mercurochrome. "You've been hurt," she said.

"I ran my bike into a tree, but I'm okay. What are you doing here?" Mark knew the answer, but he had to ask.

"My father had an accident at work." Morton had recommended this explanation until the FBI released the story.

"How is he?"

"Nothing serious, they say. He'll be home tomorrow." Ann squeezed Mark's good arm. "I got your note. It was sweet." She kissed his cheek. "Thank you."

The hospital was chilly, but Mark was flushed all over. He looked to see if anybody was watching, then kissed Ann on the lips, just the softest touch.

She smiled. "I have to get back. Maybe I'll come and see you one of these days."

"Maybe I'll come and see you."

They exchanged little waves, then Mark turned and walked toward the lobby.

Ann noticed the bag still in Mark's back pocket. "Hey, where'd you get that bag?"

Mark yanked the bag out of his pocket as he turned around. "At your house, by mistake I think, the day we took a bath and your folks came home. Where'd it come from?"

"I found it near the graveyard," she said. "I hung it on a nail in the bathroom closet and forgot about it. You can keep it if you want."

"Thanks." Mark stuffed it deep in his back pocket. He had enough troubles without explaining why he had a bank bag from the Flag Day robbery. He'd ditch it, first chance.

Ann blew Mark a kiss, and returned to her father's room.

Mark was so happy to be reconciled with Ann that he did a little jig on the way back to the lobby. Agent Cole was sitting across from Swede in an oversized chair. Mark put on a solemn face as he sat beside Swede on the sofa.

Swede jerked his thumb in Cole's direction. "The FBI, here, says we can't ever say anything about what went on tonight."

"Ever?" There went a good story for the other guys.

"National security," Cole said. "Only the bare details will be told to the press. There's a war on and if the real story got out, the enemy might profit."

Swede frowned. "Mr. Cole says that Mr. Matsui isn't a spy, that he was working for the FBI. And he's going to get a reward and maybe a medal and his picture in the paper."

"No pictures," Cole said.

"Any chance of a little reward for us?" Swede held this thumb and forefinger an inch apart.

Cole spoke through his teeth. "Reward? You almost got your eternal reward tonight."

The lobby was still. Soft bells echoed in the distance.

"How about a deal?" Swede said as he nudged Mark.

"What kind of deal?" Cole said.

"Since we can't tell anybody what happened, how about if you don't either. No sense in asking for trouble with our folks or people like Chief Morton. Mark's folks are pretty strict. And there's talk about my going to Boys Town or reform school as it is."

"I have an official report to file," Cole said.

"It seems to me," Swede said, "if you can cut the story for the papers, our part can be cut, too. You could say we were on the ridge watching the tracks being repaired. We heard the commotion when the FBI shot the Becks, but were never in any danger. We got these cuts and bruises running into trees in the woods. There aren't any witnesses except Mr. Matsui, and I'm sure he wouldn't say anything if you asked him."

Cole rubbed the stubble on his chin. "You know, Swede, going to Boys Town isn't the worst thing that could happen to you. I spent two great years there, and probably wouldn't be in the FBI otherwise." He stood up. "By the way, Father Flanagan, the founder of Boys Town, is a friend of mine. Let me know if you need a letter of introduction."

Chapter 29

Agent Cole told the boys' parents a story much like the one Swede invented. They were more relieved than angry. Mark was restricted to the Penn yard until further notice for being out after curfew.

Nobody restricted Swede. He was busy with school and Jane. Mrs. Larson had adjusted to her pregnancy, and was doing Red Cross work again.

There were newspaper headlines and radio bulletins all week about FBI raids on German-American Bund headquarters across the nation. Most had been disguised as choral, sports, and literary societies. Hundreds of members had been arrested, and the Bund was finally extinct.

The local Bund story got a headline on page one of the *Courier*, and was skimpy on details as Agent Cole had said:

BUND TRAITORS KILLED BY FBI

FBI agents raided the property of Joseph and Frederick Beck, Route 1, Middleton, Tuesday night and found evidence linking the brothers to the Flag Day robbery, the bombing of the Chicago & St. Paul rail line, and other acts of sabotage. The Becks were killed after shooting at agents. They were nephews of Heinz Beck, former regional Bund Fuhrer, who was deported to Germany a year ago.

Working undercover for the FBI and instrumental in capturing the terrorists was Robert Matsui, an American of Japanese descent who is employed by Middleton Hatchery.

When Mark entered the Aces' locker room for Saturday's practice, players stopped talking and stared at him.

Clancy charged out of his office and grabbed Mark's sleeve. "There's somebody here to see you."

"Who?"

"That's what I'd like to know. Come on."

The manager jerked Mark back to his office. A husky man in a gray baseball uniform was standing with his back to the door looking at clippings and pictures on Clancy's bulletin board. He wore a fielder's glove on his left hand and had a pair of spikes draped over his left shoulder. A gray cap stuck out of his back pocket.

"Hey, you," Clancy shouted. "The batboy's here."

The man turned around and offered his hand. "I'm John Matsui. Pleased to meet you, Mark. Ann told me all about you."

Mark shook the powerful hand. "Nice to meet you." John looked like Mr. Matsui, but he was six-feet tall and had his hair cut short in a heinie.

Clancy tapped Mark's shoulder. "He says he played for Bakersfield in the California League."

"That's what I heard," Mark said. "Played center field, hit .300. Right, John?"

"I hit .327. The league was disbanded this year because of the war."

Clancy eyed John. "What nationality are you?"

"One-hundred-percent American, born and raised in California. I can show you my birth certificate." He smiled.

"Well, never mind right now. I have to talk to the boss about this. Go out on the field. Let's see what you can do."

John nodded and jogged out the door. Mark started after him, but Clancy grabbed his arm.

"Next time ask me first. I don't like surprises."

"Honest, Clancy, I didn't know he was coming." Mark raised his right hand.

Clancy whispered, "He's Japanese, right?"

Mark nodded.

"That's just what I don't need. Other teams would have a field day. I had a cousin at Bataan. And then there's Red." He frowned.

"John's dad is the guy mentioned in the *Courier* the other day for helping the FBI break up the Bund."

"Is that so? Well, that might be a different kettle of fish. But it doesn't mean he knows anything about baseball. Still, the California League is Class C. I'll check my old *Sporting News* box scores. Sure could use a hitter now that Tommy's been drafted."

Batting practice was starting. Mark suggested to John that he go to center field. Eyebrows went up when he caught one of Whitey's drives on the warning track and hit Mark's glove on the fly at second.

Clancy stood by the dugout, hands on hips, impressed by what he saw. But could the kid hit? He yelled for John to take some cuts, and told Mark to pitch.

John threw right, but batted left. He smacked the first pitch past Mark's ear, the next one down the right field line, and the third down the left field line. All would have been hits.

Clancy told Doc to pitch. Mark stayed behind the mound to feed Doc balls. Doc threw a screwball that John missed badly. Mocking whistles came from several players. John let the next pitch go by.

Clancy hollered, "Come on, don't waste those strikes."

John crouched and waited to spring on Doc's next offering, the fastball that had sawed many bats in two. Instead of swinging, John drag-bunted the ball up the first-base line. He crossed the bag before Doc cleared the mound. John looked faster than Tommy, if that was possible.

Clancy clapped his hands. "Come on, swing away. Take your bunts later."

John dug in. Doc threw another fastball that was powered deep over the right-field fence. Swede disappeared off his perch and hustled across the parking lot after the ball.

Doc wound up and blazed another fastball. John hit it right back at Doc, who stabbed it in front of his face.

The men glared at each other. Doc came off the mound toward home plate. John dropped the bat and walked toward Doc.

Clancy spat and waddled onto the field.

Doc stuck out his hand. "I'm Doc Neal."

John grinned and shook hands. "That's some screwball you've got, Doc."

Clancy tapped John on the shoulder. "We've got a big game in Albert Lea tomorrow, and could use a guy like you in center. What d'ya say?"

John's expression turned serious. "I'll give it all I've got."

"That's all I ask."

Clancy took John by the arm, and the two headed for the manager's office to discuss terms.

Doc winked at Mark. "The kid's a natural."

Chapter 30

Ann had watched the practice from a shadowed corner in the last row of the grandstand. John had driven them to the park. It was the first time in months that they'd gone out together in public. She clasped her hands into the lap of of her blue and yellow gingham dress. Why did this little freedom seem so scary?

John had been nervous, but looked better than ever out there. Ann crossed her fingers. He and Mark seemed to hit it off, but some of the others had made faces and talked behind their gloves. She sighed.

Down by the dugout, Mark and Swede loaded bases, bats, and balls into a two-wheeled equipment cart. Ann moved down the wooden bench into the sun, called Mark's name, and waved. He waved back.

"That your Japanese girl friend?" Swede said.

"She's American. You want to meet her?"

"You kidding?"

"Well, I'm going up and talk to her. If you change your mind..."

"Fat chance." Swede pushed the cart toward the locker room.

Mark was edgy as he puffed up the long row of green steps. Nobody had seen them at the hospital, but this was different. Would others feel like Swede did?

He stopped at Ann's side. "Hi. You look nice. Going somewhere?"

"Just to see you." She smiled. "How'd John do?"

"He made the team. The owner's coming by to meet him."

"I knew you could do it."

"John did it all himself. He's just what we need to win the league again."

Mark sat beside her. Their bare arms touched. He turned toward her, thinking about a kiss, but she was frowning. "What's the matter?"

"I'm glad John can play, but I worry about how the fans'll treat him. Some were nasty in California last year, and that was before the war."

"The team'll be on his side, I think. That's half the battle."

"Don't tell anybody, but John's thinking about joining the Army."

"I thought they weren't taking any Japanese-Americans."

"They stopped after Pearl Harbor, but John heard that the Army's recruiting men in Hawaii for an all-Japanese-American unit. If they do it here, he'll enlist." Ann nudged Mark. "Did you read about my father in the paper?"

Mark nudged her back. "I guess I was right, he was a spy."

"Don't be smart. He said you could come and see me anytime."

"He did? You sure?"

Ann nodded. "He's his old self again. You know, Mayor Kern came to visit him. There's going to be an official 'Robert Matsui Day.' We've even been invited to church tomorrow. And it won't be long before school starts. I can hardly wait."

Mark nodded. He hoped that the Matsuis' passage into the community would be as easy as Ann thought.

Swede came pounding up the steps. He said to Mark, "You ready to go?"

"I want you to meet Ann first."

Ann smiled and offered her hand.

Swede glowered at her, then turned to Mark. "You coming or not?"

Ann bowed her head and bit her lip. Mark gave Swede a dirty look, which he ignored.

"I forgot to tell you," Mark said to Swede, "I'm going to the cemetery. Clancy said that they finally put up Red's headstone in the Collins plot."

Ann looked up. "That's your friend who was aboard the *Yorktown*."

"Yeah, killed by the Japanese," Swede snarled.

Ann eyed Swede. "Mark and I've been all through that. He knows that my family isn't responsible for the war, and that we're as patriotic as the next American. Right, Mark?"

"Right. That was her brother John who slugged the long one off Doc."

"I figured. Well, see you tomorrow."

"You aren't going to the cemetery?" Mark said.

"I've got things to do."

Ann stood up. "I'll go with you, Mark."

Mark gave Swede a little shrug, then Ann and he went down the steps.

Swede frowned. There was more than friendship between those two. What would Jane make of this Japanese girl? Ann Matsui would need more friends than Mark when school started. It might be interesting.

Swede started down the steps. "Hey, wait for me. I changed my mind."

Mark rode Ann double on his bike tank. If Chief Morton caught them, he'd impound the bike on the spot. Mark nuzzled Ann's soft hair and held her shoulders with his own as he steered. It might be worth losing the bike for two weeks just to see Morton's reaction to their being together.

Glenwood Cemetery lay along the south edge of Sibley Park. It was a tranquil setting of old elms, maples, and oaks that came alive again each spring with the lilacs, forsythias, and honeysuckles.

The white marble headpiece was rounded on top. The inscription was bold:

James Edward Collins
1909-1942
Killed in Action
USS Yorktown
R.I.P.

Ann knelt in the thick grass, bowed her head, and asked God to bless Red Collins. She also said a little prayer for John's safety.

Mark and Swede bowed their heads, but remained standing.

Mark remembered the last time he'd seen Red, at the Middleton train station on his way to San Diego. Why did he have to die? Why? WHY?

Swede wondered who'd visit him here if he was killed in action? Thirteen was too young to be shipped home in a box, or buried at sea. It'd break his ma's heart. Maybe he should wait awhile to enlist.

Ann stood up. There was a tear on her right cheek. Swede saw it and turned away. Mark saw it and his eyes filled with tears. Ann took Mark's hand, and leaned on his arm.

In June 1942, the Army established the 100th Infantry Battalion in Hawaii. In January 1943, they formed the 442nd Regimental Combat Team—including John Matsui—which saw action in North Africa, Italy, and France. It was one of the most highly decorated units of the war.

THE END

The Bootlegger's Secret

Michael Springer

Michael Springer
The Bootlegger's Secret

It's the summer of 1941 in Middleton, Minnesota. Eleven-year-olds Mark Penn and Swede Larson have built a treehouse along the river. School is out and the boys are looking forward to the arrival of the Ringling Brothers and Barnum & Bailey Circus, the Fourth of July parade, and the baseball season of the Middleton Aces. Mark is the team's batboy and Swede a ball shagger. One day while swimming in the river, they spot the hood ornament of a submerged 1931 Pierce-Arrow. Swede swims down, and inside the car finds an inlaid-gold cigarette case containing a music box, Turkish filter-tips, and the photograph of a beautiful woman. Later, police recover the corpse of the car's owner, Eddie Knowland, local bootlegging kingpin and member of Al Capone's Chicago gang. Knowland and his car have been missing for eight years. The cigarette case has a secret compartment containing Knowland's business records. Treasury agents want the records to prosecute corrupt officials bribed by Knowland. Chicago gangsters want the records for blackmail. When the cigarette case disappears, Mark and Swede are caught in a deadly squeeze between the T-men and the gangsters. They are not even safe at home or in their treehouse. Summer vacation becomes a nightmare of shadows and ghosts.

Learn more at:
www.outskirtspress.com/michaelspringer

LaVergne, TN USA
07 September 2010
196079LV00003B/8/P